CW00806873

"Shall I go on, Mum?"

by Peter Coath

For my wife, my daughter and my best friend

All of the events, characters and firms depicted in this book are fictitious. Any similarities to actual persons, living or dead, or actual firms, is purely coincidental.

'Even in a perfect world, where everyone is equal, I would still hold the film rights and be working on the sequel'.

Elvis Costello. Every day I Write the Book.

Part 1

Mum

"Shall I go on, Mum?"

I never wanted to write this book. That's not to say that I never wanted to write a book. Most people at some stage fantasise about writing a book and it's a common phrase that everyone has a book in them. The thing is this is not the book I planned. The book I wanted to write is a fantastical science fiction tale with magnificent twists in a universe previously unimagined. A place where people can smell colour and have senses that seek rather than just receive. Or a deep philosophical novel addressing the nature of being with an amazing insight about the nature of existence ultimately advancing our understanding of the metaphysical world. My book happens in a galaxy far far away. Apparently not. Apparently it happens in the Costa del Sol and in a small village just outside of Dunstable.

My book is about my mum. Actually no. My book is about my mother's illness and the enormous effect that it had on her, but more than that on all around her. By that you might be expecting a sad and sympathetic story of illness, a heart wrenching tale of a battle fought against the odds with high and low points, laughter and tears and ultimately a sad but poignant end. No. Well partly yes but so much more than that. The story I have to tell actually happened. Everyone loves a true story except those who actually live them. What follows might be and in fact hopefully is entertaining but it was also my life and I actually went through everything that I am about to write. Like I said I never intended to write this and just for the record it happened over a year ago so it's likely to be a bit sketchy. I didn't keep a diary of events. I have probably forgotten or misremembered most of what happened. But it did happen. I am not doing it for cathartic reasons. The strangest thing about living in the world of the bizarre is that it may be bizarre but it is all very real. People have said to me that it will be good to get it down on paper, a chance to get it out of my system. No it won't. It was shit the first time and it will be shit the second time but I am going to do it anyway. I am also not doing it so the world will know my plight. I am very much aware that you all have enough going on in your own lives to care about me. It's a bit like when people show you photos of themselves on holiday with people you have never met and have absolutely no interest in. You know, in the old days it would be in the form of actual photos but now people scroll through the camera roll on their phones saying "This is Trevor and Julie, this is Trevor and Julie by the entrance to our apartment, this is Trevor falling over on the dance floor. I have never met nor am I likely to meet Trevor and Julie and as a result have absolutely no interest whatsoever of looking at photos of, not to put too fine a point on it, strangers.

The reason that I am writing this book is because I am lazy. I am doing it because it is so much easier to recount your life than create a world of a desert planet or a world of wizards or dragons. That takes a lot of effort and imagination where as if I simply recount what has gone before I just have to remember it and then write it down. Oh I do have to go through the whole thing again which if I am honest is not a prospect that I am looking forward to. The other reason that I am writing this book is because when it was happening I lost count of the amount of people who said you should write a book about this, if you didn't know that it actually happened you wouldn't believe it. And they say write about what you know, so here goes. This is not my book. But apparently it is.

Ch 1. Coming Home

It all started in September 2012 in the most mundane way
possible. I was standing outside of SuperTyre's, talking to my
Mum on the mobile whilst pacing backwards and forwards. I
do this now when I am on the phone, I never used to in the old
days but this is probably because back then phones had
cables. If you walked backwards and forwards you would
eventually rip the phone off of the wall. I was pacing on a
rough piece of land on what had turned out to be a relatively
clement day, watching the various cars and lorries going about
their business on the dual carriageway that is the Dunstable
road. My mother was somewhere different entirely, in the
front room of her three story semi-detached house in
Marbella, Spain. She moved to Spain when my parents split
up some fifteen years previously. Mum found a pair of
another woman's underpants in the laundry basket and so
confronted my Dad who admitted to having an affair, thus
causing the split. I sometimes wonder what would have
happened if Mum had decided to turn a blind eye. She could
have put the pants in the bin and pretended they were never
there, or that they had actually been hers and she had got
confused. Can you do such a thing? I suppose that it depends
on the individual. Mum couldn't. Or maybe she had hoped
for a different outcome. Hoped that Dad would admit to
having a fling but that it meant nothing, that he was sorry and
could they make another go of things. The first part was true.
But he didn't say that it was just a fling, in fact he told my
Mum that he was in love with someone else and as a result of

this they split up. I come from a family of market traders who made good money back in the eighties, a time where you could go to work with a bucket of air and come home with a few hundred quid in your pocket and as a result alongside our house in England we also had a flat in Spain. This is where Mum decided to make her life. Why Spain and not England we will come to later. Probably. I'm going off-piste.

So as I said I was outside Super Tyres getting a tyre for the van and I decided to take advantage of the twenty-five-minute wait to call Mum. This would be expensive, calling Spain from a mobile but it had one major advantage. It meant that I could ring my mother from outside the house. The reason this was preferable and I probably should confess this early is because my mother was a pain in the arse. I loved her because she was my mother. She had always been a loving mother and she had done a fairly good job of raising me, but she was still a pain in the arse. It wasn't that she was nasty she just exhibited many of the traits that I don't value highly in individuals. Our conversation would always start in the same way. I would ask her how she was and she would tell me. Or more specifically I would say "how are you mum?" and she would say "well I've got flu at the moment and I've got a pain in my leg." There was always something wrong with her, despite the fact that there was never anything wrong with her.

Furthermore, when you talked to her you could tell that she wasn't really listening. Instead she was working out a way to turn the conversation around to something that she wanted to talk about and it was always about someone else. If I were to say that Molly (my daughter and her only granddaughter) has done really well in her exams at school she wouldn't say "that's great, tell her I said well done". No. Her response would be something like "Sheila's daughter Sophie came second in the swimming competition". I'm sure she did and I am very happy for her but bearing in mind that I hardly know Sheila's daughter what are you telling me this for? I always presumed that she was the same with everyone but to be honest, I am not so sure. I think that she tried really hard with people that she didn't really know so as to earn their approval and was complacent with her true friends and family because these are the people that she knew would be there for her anyway.

I say that she never listened but that's not actually true. I would tell her about what I was doing and then she would criticise me for doing it wrong. Or I would tell her that I had been out for dinner with Lisa's family and she would go quiet because I hadn't included her, despite the fact that she was nearly fifteen hundred miles away. It got to the stage where our telephone conversations often descended into silence because every time I thought of something to say, I instantly thought 'no I had better not say that, it will upset her.' Honestly by the end of a fifteen-minute phone call I would feel quite rung out.

And another thing, if you asked her for something her first word was always no. No big deal most people's first word is always no. I remember the first time I realised it. I realised that it was one of the games that the two of us played. I was about twelve at the time and I had asked my Mum if I could have a lift to the Bath Road swimming baths in our home town of Luton. I knew before I had uttered the question what her reply would be because her automatic answer was always no. Then what I would have to do was ask repeatedly until she would eventually cave in. You know the kind of thing.

"Can I have a lift to swimming mum?"

"No".

"Pleeease".

"No, I'm busy".

The conversation would continue like a war of attrition until eventually she would say yes and then give me a lift to the baths with the hump. On this particular day I had a revelation. I saw a shortcut to the end. I asked her if I could have a lift and when she said no I said "don't worry, I'll get the bus". I didn't want to get the bus. Who wants to get the bus? You have to wait for the bus, busses are slow and go the long way round. Cars take you straight to your destination. Cars are warm and comfortable. Cars have music. Even if it is Chris de Burgh. But there comes a time in every man's life when you have to take a stand and what's more I knew that that is exactly what I wasn't doing. I knew exactly what was going to happen. I came bounding down the stairs with a rolled up towel under my arm to find my Mum standing in the hallway holding her keys saying "Do you want a lift or not?"

Now let's face it, this automatically saying no is hardly the crime of the century and I will bet you a pound to a penny that this has happened to you. It's most people's default answer. It was just a game that we both played. Another one of our games was when we sat down to dinner it always ended up in a debate/row. This situation was not helped by the fact that my parents were both Thatcherite Tories and I was a student wanker. Family Sunday dinners degenerated into political debates about the plight of the homeless or gypsies or any of the usual bollocks with me automatically gainsaying what she said and vice versa until my Dad got bored and left the table to watch Antiques Roadshow or something equally mundane. Then our conversations drew to a halt. It's no fun without an audience.

Despite all of our differences I still loved my mother and I had good reason to. My mother fell pregnant at the age of seventeen and I was an unplanned pregnancy. My Mum and Dad did their best to make a go of it, living with my grandparents but my Dad couldn't hack it and left when I was about two. This may have had a dramatic effect on my formative years but to be honest at the age of two I had only just about worked out which way was up and so I was not familiar with the concept of a nuclear family. I was raised by my Mum and my grandparents or more particularly my Grandma. My Grandad worked the track at Vauxhall alongside the entire population of the rest of the town. Mum worked at Kents. Kents was one of those typical offices that you got in the seventies. In retrospect I imagine a place where everything was made of brown or orange corduroy and the boss sat behind an enormous desk with a blotting pad, smoking cigarettes and groping his secretary. Mum worked there as an eighteen-year-old girl with a full time job and a baby to look after. This she did with the help of my Grandma. My Grandma was not everyone's cup of tea. She managed to acquire the nickname 'whinging Wyne' because her name was Winifred and she never stopped moaning. In her defence she had always suffered from bad health as a child and it is difficult to be upbeat when you are in constant pain. She may have not been everyone cup of tea but she loved me. Bearing in mind the age gap between us and the fact that I lived with my grandparents it was like having a son and grandson at the same time. That level of love is tangible. I honestly believe that I could have committed genocide and Grandma would have told me they asked for it.

Then when I was about five Mum managed to get us a flat and the two of us moved out. I think that was a tremendous wrench for my Grandma but at the end of the day it was me and Mum and we would be living together. The flat was on an estate in what was one of the worst areas of Luton called Marsh Farm. It had been built in the seventies when contemporary designers were experimenting with all of the different and unusual things that you can do with concrete. It was the time of 'high rises' but luckily for us we were on of the lucky ones and lived on the ground floor of a two story flat. And the thing is as a kid you don't think of it as a poverty stricken estate, you think of it as home. It was warm and dry and had electric lighting and running water, more than many people have even now. Mum carried on working at Kents and I became a latch key kid. I spent my days at school and my evenings riding around the estate on my Raleigh

Grifter. Circling the estate and the blocks of garages then back under the underpass, home. I can honestly say that I have never been happier. I would return to the flat for dinner which Mum would make every night. She was a good cook and although we didn't have much to live on she always made a decent meal. Like salad. In the seventies salad consisted of: corned beef; grated cheese; lettuce: tomato (cut in the shape of a water lily) and cucumber. Oh and salad cream, that made the whole thing palatable. However It wasn't always salad. She made the best ever steak and kidney pie, with two different kinds of pastry and her deserts were out of this world. My favourite was pineapple upside down cake but I am a philistine and some of the stuff she created could easily give the mob on 'bake off' a run for their money. In the evenings Mum would play Motown or Kate Bush on the record player and I would listen and play with my Lego. She was a twenty-three-year-old girl woman, alone with a child of five and running a flat whilst holding down a full time job. She never complained and took the whole thing in her stride and we were happy together.

Still things for Mum were about to get easier. Dad reappeared on the scene. Mum and Dad started seeing each other again and he moved in. Mum had to keep it from my grandparents, who were understandably not best pleased with Dads less than supportive behaviour and who had expected that Dad would reappear again, just because Mum now had her own place. This may well have been true; but it is also true that it is hard to have a proper married relationship whilst living under someone else's roof, particularly if that roof belongs to your in-laws. As it turned out older is not always wiser and my grandparents' fears were unfounded. Dad stayed around for the next twenty-five years and if only he could have kept his nob in his pants he may well have been there at the end of what would have turned out to be a very different and significantly less painful story. Suffice to say that for a while it was just me and Mum and we were happy. I think that we always fought but so does the rest of the world. There are worst things. There are children in Africa starving, get over it.

It's no secret that the bond between a mother and her son is a special kind of bond. The thing about children is that you create a new life, nurture it and craft it, hopefully, into a well-rounded individual. A bit like cutting a perfect diamond and when your diamond is glistening and shining in the glory of the midday sun, then another woman comes and takes him away. That's bound to cause at least a little resentment. Before we go on I don't think that me comparing myself to a diamond is egotistical. After all, I am very bright.

Ch.2 Lisa

At this point I would like to introduce my wife and so our story fast forwards about twenty years. I was always a bit of a fat kid in school. My Mum fed me portions the size of my Dad's because I was a growing lad. Yeah growing sideways. I still stayed with my Grandma from Friday night through to Saturday to give my parents some time together and she bought me jumbo bags of crisps and cakes which I would scoff in-between breakfast and lunch. Then luckily for me when I hit fourteen I had somewhat of a growth spurt. My waist pushed upward and I became six foot one and thin as a rake. The problem with this is that in your mind's eye you still see yourself as the fat kid that you were growing up. Special K used to do an add on the tele that said that if you can 'pinch more than an inch' then you need the Special K diet. I spent most of the mid-eighties pinching my midriff convinced that I bore a strong resemblance to a weeble.

In everyday life I was extremely confident. As I have said I was the son of a market trader. As my Dad's business grew we got a stall on Milton Keynes market which was run by my Mum and my Grandma. I continued to stay with my Grandma on the Friday night but then on the Saturday morning Mum would pick us up in the Volkswagen LT35 van and off we would go to work. Hanging around a shopping centre for twelve hours at the age of eleven wasn't exactly the most engaging of activities. I managed to relieve my boredom by getting a job on 'Geoff's records' the stall behind. I used to stand on an upturned orange crate, so that I could see over the huge stack of LP's and pitch Billy Jo Spears or Chas and Daves Jamboree bag to unsuspecting punters. A particular favourite was Geoff Love's Banjo Party. A load of old age pensioners singing war songs while some bloke played the banjo. "All your favourites, all the old ones, all the gold ones, all in a gate fold sleeve." I was always an exhibitionist anyway: 'everybody look at me', with the job on the records my confidence shot through the roof. Yet when it came down to talking to women, on a scale of one to ten my confidence was less than zero.

My work on the record stall was of absolutely no help when on a particular fateful Friday night, me and the boys walked into our usual drinking haunt Chicago's. Chicago's was situated on George Street, the road that contained all of the main pubs were in Luton. They were all practically next to each other which was handy because it meant that if you decided to go on a pub crawl you didn't have to walk very far. It hadn't been open that long and it was like no other pub in the street, it was an American fun pub. It had Budweiser on tap, an American beer that has no flavour whatsoever. There were American licence plates attached to American cars that protruded from the walls. It played the soundtrack from Grease and from time to time 'Dave double decks the DJ' would encourage us to look at the video screens which were showing a clip it from the Wombles. In retrospect it sounds like the definition of hell. We were there practically every night.

On the night in question the pub had a new welcome addition. At the bar was an angel. I couldn't miss her as she was right in front of me as I walked through the door. She was sitting on a bar stool with two of her girlfriends, one on either side of her. She had alabaster skin, curly red hair down to her waist and she was and still is the most beautiful thing I have seen in my life. I felt that I had been struck by lightning. Now I know people use that phrase and I'm sure that if it has never happened to you, you probably think 'does that really happen or is it just something that people say to be melodramatic?' Well I can categorically tell you that it does. I know because it happened to me. You don't have to believe me, you've already bought the book, I've got your money, what do I care? For those of you who are in a relationship and didn't feel like a bolt of lightning hit you the very second you saw your spouse don't worry, I'm sure that you will still be fine and for those of you who did, great isn't it? Confronted by the radiant red head in front of me I did what I always did when confronted by beautiful women and totally fell to pieces.

The rest of the night then degenerated into one of those 20 go to 10 subroutines that we used to type into basic computers in the early 80's. You know when you got your Sinclair spectrum and to try to convince your parents that it wasn't just a machine for playing games (it was, Manic Miner and Jet Set willy to be precise) you would write a program. If you can call it a program that is because it was only two lines long:

10 Print "Gary smells of cheese"

```
20 Goto 10
```

```
Run
```

The whole screen would then scroll 'Gary smells of cheese". Hell I was practically as good a programmer as Mathew Broderick in War Games. On the night in question my sub routine went like this:

```
10 Get a pint and talk to the beautiful girl

20 Drink pint first to gain enough courage to talk to the
beautiful girl

30 Go to the toilet to drain pint and then talk to the beautiful
girl

40 On the way back from toilet Goto 10
```

In my heart of hearts I knew that it wasn't going to happen. I would never have the courage to approach such a beautiful creature. It's not just the rejection, although that would be crushing enough. It was more the fact that she would confirm what I already knew, that she was way out of my league. Better to wonder wistfully what might have been than know for a fact that this would never be mine. Besides the way I was going by the time that I had enough Dutch courage to talk to her I would be pissed and then she would just think who's the drunken prat. Budwieser may taste like water but it's still five per cent. Please drink responsibly.

Looking back on it I think that fate lent a hand. I think the same force that brings the lightening is the one that is predestined to bring you together, if that makes any sense. Thing is that after exiting the toilet for what must have been about the fifth time, there she was, up near the corner table by the window where I had previously been standing, talking to my best mate. Now I love Nigel. I have known him since I was eleven and at the age of forty-six we are still the best of friends but he was batting way above his average, by definition would anyone be. I found out later that he had gone up to talk to her. I wouldn't have had the nerve. Obviously. But thank god he did and for that reason alone I am forever in his debt. I did what any true friend would do. I walked straight up to the two of them, pushed Nige out of the way, stuck out my hand to the redhead and said "Hi my names Pete". Nige looked a tad perturbed, no actually it was more like thoroughly pissed off but fuck him there were cosmic forces at work here. The three of us spoke for the rest of the evening and then we left. There was no way that I would ever have had the courage to ask for her number and so I made my way home safe in the knowledge that I would never see the most beautiful girl in the world again. Me and Nige walked home along the disused railway track that connected the town centre with Leagrave, the part of Luton where we lived. It was a funny end to the evening. I knew that I would never see her again but I had spent the last part of the evening with an angel and I was happy that I had spoken to her. She was nice.

After the weekend was over I went back to college. I was studying Public Administration at Teesside Polytechnic. Why go there to do that course? Why do you think, I got really bad A level grades. If they ever advertised the advert should say: Teesside Polytechnic Social Sciences department, the place of choice for the educationally challenged, get to us via clearing because let's face it we're never going to be your first choice. I am being overly harsh, Middlesbrough is a great place, the people are lovely and I had a great time there and learned a lot, albeit not about administration. Two weeks later I was standing in the kitchen of my shared student house, a dwelling that made the Young Ones house look like a Barratt show home, when the phone rang. It was Nige. After the usual greeting the conversation quickly turned to Nigel's latest news.

"Guess who I am taking out?" said Nige

"No idea". I replied although this is not strictly true. There would only be one person who it could be although I had no idea how.

"You know that red haired girl that we met in the pub".

Bastard! He's ringing up to gloat. In all fairness if I were in his position I would have done exactly the same thing. And you've got to admire his inventiveness. Remember this was in an age before technology. He had gone down to the town hall, got her address from the electoral register and put a rose on her doorstep with a note that said 'would you come out to dinner with me'. He may be a bastard but he was a bastard with a whole lot of style. Nige and Lisa went out a few times but it never really took off as a relationship, it was more of a friend thing. Still while they were kind of dating there was no way that I could ask Lisa out. It's one of the unwritten rules is that you don't go out with your mate's sisters and you don't go out with your mate's girlfriends. Thing is I really liked this girl and she wasn't actually his girlfriend. It had to happen. I waited for about three months. I'm not a complete shit. Then when I was sure that there was nothing going on between them, I asked Lisa out. From the very beginning our love was tangible. Like I say I believe that it was meant to be. There was only one obstacle. Mum.

I wouldn't say that they didn't get on it's just that my Mum was incredibly difficult. By way of example here are just a couple of some of Mum's prize one liners.

"You'll never be as thin as your friend".

Nice, and later on after Lisa had fallen pregnant with Molly:

 "That's not all baby".

Now bearing in mind that as a young girl Lisa had developed a minor eating disorder was this really the way forward?

She was also a wind up. That was the culture in the eighties, particularly on the markets. It was the time of Game for a Laugh. She once gave my friend Gary such a hard time about writing a phone number on the front of our copy of the yellow pages and then tearing it off a bit of the cover that he

21

refused to come to my front door to knock for me. Instead he sent Nige up to the door while he waited at the bottom of the driveway. Apparently they always wrote numbers on the front of the yellow pages and tore it off in their house. He did get his own back though. He came in (about a month later when he had lifted his embargo) with a brand spanking new page he had obtained from a virgin copy of the yellow book and blu tacked it onto the front of ours. I always liked Gary, he sees the world differently to most.

Thing is none of my Mum's traits were ever the crime of the century, they were just annoying. Mum was never out and out nasty but she would do things that would leave you asking 'what did you do that for?' And as I said, there was always something wrong with her. Mum never worked out that 'how are you' is actually a statement and not a question. I would call and say 'how are you?' and rather than what you are supposed to say "I'm fine Pete, how are you?" instead I would get a full diagnosis of everything that she thought was wrong with her. There was nothing wrong with her. She craved the attention and sympathy that comes with ill health. Be careful what you wish for.

Ch.3 Dave

So on the occasion in question when I was doing my weekly phone call from outside Super Tyre's and I asked her how she was and she told me that she didn't feel herself, I did not fall over backwards aghast at the situation. Mum went on to explain that she was having trouble saying certain words. Although her mind knew what it wanted to say the words would not come out of her mouth. Now you can call me unsympathetic if you like but you have to bear in mind that me and Mum had quite a history of her annotating her ailments, while I had perfected the ability to switch off. I believe at some stage we have all done it. We have been on the phone to someone and whilst they were in the throes of a full paced monologue, took the phone away from our ear, raised our heads towards the sky and chanted silently to ourselves 'here we go again'. In this instance however I was kind of paying attention. I was fully aware of my mother's leanings towards hypochondria but this really didn't sound right. Then again, it was probably nothing to worry about, maybe the early onset of dementia. Happens when you get older. I tried to be sympathetic and said that she shouldn't worry too much but that it would probably be wise to get it checked out. Mum had concluded that perhaps she had a mini stroke, dementia was clearly not a grand enough illness and that she was coming home to have a full check-up at BUPA.

My parents were always staunch conservatives. This was not an ethical or philosophical stance. It had nothing to do with the ethos of laissez faire government or an abhorrence or the nanny state and a staunch belief in the individual's right to choose. No what it was to do with was around the mid nineteen eighties Nigel Lawson reduced the top rate of income tax to 40 percent, thus saving them a fucking fortune. With this in mind they also bought into everything else that conservative philosophy dictated. My Mum wanted to send me to private school but I was heavily against it on the grounds that: all my mates went to the local comprehensive; the local private school looked shit and I didn't want to turn into a complete nob. If you have been to private school, I apologise. I'm not apologising in case I have offended you, I'm just sorry. My Dad who was less nouveaux riche than Mum backed me up. He did however enrol us all in BUPA. I had myself removed from Bupa about four years later. I had been at Sixth form college for over a year and so the stick on socialist in me had become fully functional. I also made a good case. I was eighteen, fully fit and they were just wasting their money. I didn't have to ask them twice.

Mum was coming home. She would come home for a week or two and during this time I booked her in at the holiday cottages down the road known as Bellows Mill. Bellows Mill is a fantastic place. It is run by a lady called Rachel and it has been in her family for generations. Rachel and her family live in the main house and all of the outbuildings have been converted into little holiday lets some of which are quirky (one is called the love shack and I know for a time they even had a yurt) all set on acres of ground with a great big lake in the middle. It's idyllic. It also meant that Mum had her own front door, her own independence and the added advantage that during her stay we wouldn't kill each other of which there was always a high probability if we stayed under the same roof.

As well as returning for the check-up Mum also wanted to come back because Derick was getting on her nerves. Derick was Mums long-time boyfriend. Since leaving Dad and moving to Spain Mum's life had taken various twists and turns. She quickly became aware that when you move from the position of someone's wife to that of a single woman, you cease to get invited out. This is partly because it might make the numbers odd or that it might alter the dynamic but it is mainly because women make the arrangements and women regard other women, particularly single women as a threat. In all fairness they are probably right. I knew a woman whose girlfriend had split up with her husband and had nowhere to go so she put her up for a while. Six months later the new lodger ran off with her husband. No good turn goes unpunished. I mean there is nothing to say that a married woman might be after your husband but the chances are lower if they have a partner and hopefully they are happy. Like the joke goes: 'What do men and women have in common? They both hate women'. Tell that to a man and he will laugh. Tell it to a woman and she just nods. My mate Nige calls women snakes with tits. My wife agrees.

As it was Mum found a good friend in a lady called Lucy. Lucy is a bright well-presented lady who was in the same boat as my Mum. Lucy is kind of posh. By that I mean she speaks correctly in that RP English that everyone on the BBC used to use in the seventies. She has no accent. She is always well turned out, she sits correctly, she is never rude but at the same time will make her point known but without ever overstepping the mark. Lucy is a lady. Fortunately for my Mum she was a single lady and two ladies together are no longer a threat but rather their own little social group. They went out together. They drank too much. Mum started smoking for the first time in twenty odd years. They had fun. Then Mum met Dave.

Dave was a fat pale man with short curly ginger hair (I've got nothing against red heads, my wife is a red head). He was also a man with very few, sorry no, social graces. However, he did have his own villa with a pool, a large expensive Mercedes, a boat and his own Mazda import business. Therein lay the problem. Dave was a self-made man. He had worked from nothing and now earned a fortune importing cars from Japan. Unfortunately, he was one of those people for whom the trappings of that kind of wealth also brought arrogance. He was the kind of man who would click his fingers at waiters. Never let people out at junctions because he had the better car and it was his right of way. It's kind of like you get with pop stars. They spend so long surrounded by people telling them that they are fantastic and laughing at their jokes that after a while they seem to think that they are some kind of god. Dave was like that. He was rude, obnoxious, tight, and generally unpleasant. And now he was going out with my Mum. Yay!

Partly in defence of her terrible taste in a boyfriend, Mum had been used to money. Like I said market traders in the eighties did alright. Don't believe everything you see on fools and horses, we didn't all live in Nelson Mandela house.

As a matter of fact, during my teenage years we lived in a house called 'The Grange'. It was a detached Victorian six-bedroom house in an acre of land with a snooker room that had space for two tables and its own tennis court. It was fabulous. I'm not telling you this to brag in any way, I'm just trying to explain that Mum was used to luxury. She lived in a big house. They had a new Range Rover. They went on cruses every year at a time when not everyone did cruises. And fair play to her. She had always been there to support my Dad and in fact Milton Keynes, the market that my Mum and Grandma ran two days a week was one of our busiest. It was the life that she had had, the life that she had made until another woman came and took it out from under her and left her in a foreign land without her husband. See, snakes with tits. Also Mum was lonely. It can be hard enough being single when you always have been but Mum had been married for twenty-seven years. She missed company and I suppose she thought that bad company was better than none.

Dave could give my Mum everything that she had previously had with my Dad. Security and a lifestyle to which she had become accustomed. Problem was that Dave was a bit of a shit but that didn't seem to bother my Mum. Mum and Dave lived in his villa in Spain, just outside Marbella and from time to time they would fly back to England. On the flight home Dave would orchestrate an argument with my mother. She would come home and I would say: "Aren't you seeing Dave while you're at home mum?" Or "I thought Dave was coming over and we were going out for dinner?" She would tell me that on the flight home they had had a massive barney and they weren't talking. Then, two days before they were due to fly back he would ring her up to tell her that he was sorry and they would make up and fly back together. Every time. Strange behaviour indeed.

Dave had a mole growing on his back. Fair skin and a Spanish sun are not a good mix, particularly when they are accompanied by the kind of arrogance that goes hand in hand with "I don't need suntan lotion." This is the kind of arrogance me amigo, that gets you killed. Sure enough Dave's mole was undercover cancer, a cancer that turned out to be terminal. It's a funny word terminal. I have never worked out why you would use the same word to describe the place where you wait for a plane and certain death. Surely not the image that you are trying to instil in people who are about to get into a large metal cigar tube with wings and launch themselves thirty thousand feet up in the air. The doctors told Dave that he didn't have long to live and he didn't want to die in Spain so he returned to England. This time he didn't have a row with Mum. How could he? Besides bearing in mind what he was going through, even if they did have a fight, there was no way that Mum was not going to be with her long term partner when the time came. And so she was. On his death bed my mother was there right by his side. On the other side of the bed was his wife. Turned out that the reason that Dave always orchestrated a fight on the plane was because he had two women on the go. Wife in England (who he rarely came home to by the way) and my Mum, a girlfriend in Spain. The whole thing sounds like an early eighties sitcom. Music by Ronnie Hazlehurst. I told you he was a shit. This really happened. Honestly I could be making this stuff up but I'm not and I'm only warming up. On the plus side of things, me and Lisa did get a Mazda out of him. A white Mazda 323 with electric windows and alloy wheels. It wasn't any cheaper than it would have been in a showroom. Mum lent me the money to buy it.

With Dave off of the scene Mum was only single for a short amount of time before a new beau entered the arena. Now I should say that my mother was a good looking woman. In photos of her on her wedding day she bore more than a passing resemblance to a young Elizabeth Taylor. Just with a bump. If you look closely you can see me waving. I am very lucky that Mum passed on at least half of her genes on to me. It's not that my Dad's side are ugly but some of them had more chins than the 'Aquaphibians' from Stingray. The new suitor was a gentleman from the golf club called Derick Pirozzoli. Derick was unfortunate in many ways. He is a short man, shorter than my mother who herself was only around five foot six. He is very hairy all over his entire body except for on his head. This he compensates for by taking what hair he does have, growing it long on one side and sweeping it over his bald pallet giving him a style similar to that sported by seventies football managers. Now you can't help your genetics but on top of it all he was kind of, well, grubby. He never smelt but you got the feeling that he maybe could have changed his clothes a little more often. Rather than changing his underpants he would turn them round. Then inside out. Then round again. Mum said that she had to practically prize them off him to get them in the wash.

Derick may have been grubby, and short, and hairy but he did listen. His social graces may not have been the greatest but he did have them. He would tell stories about his youth growing up as an Italian Scot in Glasgow. His father was an ice cream man and in turn he and his brothers had also taken to the vans. He didn't have a Mercedes or a boat but he did have a bar in fish alley Fengirola and a couple of flats. He was Catholic and tee total and as a result his views were sometimes pious and sanctimonious but let's face it, he wasn't Dave.

Mum and Derick were happy together for quite a few years. It's funny that when you look back it is hard to put a timeframe on exactly how long it was but I would guess that they were together for the best part of ten years, maybe more. During this time Mum sold her flat in Spain and used this money with the help of a mortgage obtained either by Derick or by the two of them together (if she ever spoke finances I just switched off, it was her money she could do what she liked) and they bought a three story town house near Cabopino. My mother and Derick had a life together. She worked long hours in the bar, cooking in a hot and tiny kitchen and she would complain that Derick was tight and driving her mad. From time to time they would fall out. She would call me and tell me that she needed a break or that she had had enough and she was going to leave him. She would come home for a week or two but she always went back. I'm sure that it was not all one sided. Let's not forget that Derick had to put up with my mother and she was a very difficult woman. Have I mentioned that?

They also had many good times together. They took long holidays playing golf in Thailand or South Africa, even in Scotland. In all fairness if you're not in Edinburgh or Glasgow all there is to do in Scotland is drill for oil, shoot defenceless animals and play golf. Me and Lisa toured the Highlands of Scotland on our honeymoon. It was shut. After one such holiday Mum and Derick stopped off in England before returning to Spain and announced that they were getting married. We were really pleased for them. The wedding would be in Spain which made sense because that is where all of their friends and Derick's family were. I pictured myself wearing a linen suit or even a kilt although in all honesty in a full tartan affair I would have been a bit warm in the Spanish sun. I need not have worried though. On returning to Spain the matter was broached with Derick's two daughters and the subject became somewhat cooler. They told their dad in no uncertain terms that he had been married twice previously and they did not want him to make the same mistake again. None taken. Also Derick has a heart condition and if Mum became Mrs Pirozzoli then she would stand to inherit the bar and the flats. I'm sure that ultimately they had their dads interests at heart and I am not saying that they were in any way concerned for their inheritance.

Yes I am.

Ch.4 Coming home (again)

Mum returned to England. I can't really call it coming home because for the best part of fifteen years she had lived in Spain so that's an inappropriately named chapter. Twice. She safely ensconced herself in Bellows Mill and we invited her round for dinner. We always did that on the first night she came home and we always got a Chinese, the same Chinese. It was the one that we would get when I was a young boy and me and Dad had gone to work on the bank holiday. We worked on a market called Fordham. It was in a farmer's field which for 361 days of the year had cows in it but for of the four bank holidays it became a market. We put a shovel in the back of the van for the obvious reason. Mum would bake fresh rolls and fill them with tinned salmon for our lunch and we always ate them before we had even got out of the van. When we got home Dad would go to the Jade House in Leagrave and pick up a Chinese for dinner, back in the days when you only got a takeaway on special occasions and we always had the same thing. While I am not convinced that: chicken in batter, prawn balls, special fried rice, a prawn omelette covered in sweet and sour sauce and a portion of chips is the kind of meal you would expect to find in the average far eastern household, that is what we had. The night Mum returned home she stayed for the evening, drank a little too much as usual but all in all the evening was pleasant. To be honest there didn't seem to be too much wrong with her. Okay so she couldn't recall the odd word and from time to time had to stop to compose what it was that she wanted to say but I can't say that it was obvious. If she hadn't mentioned that there was something wrong, I honestly don't think that I would even have noticed. Lisa agreed. She said that she didn't think that there was anything wrong with her and that her inability to recall words seemed to increase as the evening went on so it was probably drink related. To me she just felt like Mum just with the odd missing word. Like a 1000-piece jigsaw with a few pieces missing. It may be incomplete but you still know what the picture is.

Over the next few days' Mum would spend her days doing the usual stuff, stuff you do when you live in Spain and come home to England. Buying cheap coffee and tea from Asda. Purchasing pink and peach oversized t shirts from Marks and Spencer and comfortable shoes from Clarks. Basically killing time until her BUPA health check. In the evenings on the way home from work I would call in and we would have a glass of wine together and talk about our days. She would miss words and I would take the piss or put thoroughly inappropriate words in the spaces and she would laugh and tell me to shut up.

On the day of the health check Mum drove over to BUPA on her own. I was working and Lisa offered to accompany her but she said that it wasn't necessary as it was just a check-up and besides
it was only around the corner. We said 'fine, come for your tea when you are finished.' When I got back from work that day Mum was already here. The good news was that they didn't think it was a mini stroke. This meant that I had to stop my impersonations of Helen Daniels from neighbours which

is probably for the best as I didn't really watch neighbours and they weren't very good anyway. The people at BUPA said that it could be a number of thing's and that they wanted to send her up to Queens College in London for a full MRI scan.

Now I should state at this point that people and hospitals fit into two different categories: those who think that you go into hospital to get better and those who think that you go into hospital to die. I think whichever category you belong to depends on your life experience. I am the former. I broke my ankle running down stairs at the age of sixteen. I went to hospital and the doctors fixed it. Lisa got pregnant, went into hospital with a bump in her tummy and a baby came out. All good. Admittedly both my grandparents went in to hospital and came out dead but they were old and old people die, it's not the hospitals fault. My Mum having similar life experiences as me shared my belief and being relatively young and still very able what is the worst thing that could happen?

Having said that because of the situation had now escalating to the next level we were all of the belief that Derick should return home for moral support and we all knew how that would go. Derick's initial response was that he couldn't come because he had no one to run the bar. Kind of a weak argument under the circumstances. After all, if you were going for a full MRI scan I'm guessing that you would want your partner to be there, even if you weren't getting along that well at the moment. Kind of a morality thing really. As it was Derick was a mild man. I'm not sure if he was weak willed or if he was just the kind who wanted a quiet life. Actually I'm not sure if there is a difference. In addition, he was surrounded by very forthright women. My mother could be forthright and he had two daughters who were both outspoken especially his eldest, Linda who was one of those people who believed that they could say exactly what they wanted, whenever they wanted because it was their opinion and they were entitled to voice it. I personally don't agree with this philosophy. In my opinion people have feelings and need to be treated with consideration. I gave up the belief that I am right all of the time and that everyone wants to hear what I have to say when I was twelve. It was from the daughters that the second line of defence came. Their dad was ill and shouldn't travel with his heart condition. Again nonsense. They were booked on a cruise in January how were they going to get to the ship? Teleport? Also you can fly halfway round the world to play golf but you can't fly the fifteen hundred miles to be with the woman who would have been your wife, please.

In the end Derick acquiesced. I think that he just listened to reason. Mum said she needed him so he had to be there. He told his daughters, they were not happy but they would just have to live with it. And so Derick flew into Luton in time to go with my mother to The National Hospital of Neurology and Neurosurgery, Queens Square London.

Ch.5 Oh God

You know when you get those situations where everything is the same but actually everything is different. I had one once when we had just got back from a family holiday to America. We came back to the house somewhat jet lagged but fine and very quickly Lisa's parents came round. They don't normally do this. There is normally about an hour or two before people start to appear which gives us time to acclimatise to being back in normal life. They asked about our holiday and everything seemed normal but somehow I got the sense that something was different. Then my mother-in-law said "Peter, I've got some bad news, your Auntie Sue's dead." At first I thought my Auntie Sue up north who I saw rarely and although she was not old she was not young either. Then the penny dropped. She meant my Auntie Sue who lived round the corner, my Auntie who was in her late forties and did moon walks for charity, my Auntie who had four kids. I remember my response. I said "Fuck off" and then "No" that's what you blurt out when you are in a place of total disbelief. Then the news slowly sinks in. You think about the consequences and you adapt.

I came home from work that Wednesday night, the night of Mums' scan. I walked through the door and shouting 'hello', just like I did on any other night. I walked into the main room to find Lisa sitting at the table and Mum Derick and Mum hovering around the breakfast bar wall that separates the kitchen from the dining room. Everyone asked me how my day had been and I said that everything was fine.

36

I was wrong, it wasn't. It was at that point that Lisa said "I think you had better sit down".

Turns out it definitely wasn't a stroke. No, it was a large Malignant grade 4 brain tumour situated right in the middle of her brain and it was terminal. I don't really know where to go with that.

Still you have to go somewhere so we sat around the table and we talked about what the doctors had said and what might possibly happen. Then something very surreal happened. I got up to go to the toilet and when I came out Derick was standing there in the hallway, waiting for me. He asked if he could have a word in private so we hovered in the corridor. Then he said: "Peter we have got a bit of a problem. The thing is because we are not married under the law in Spain if your mother dies then the house automatically reverts to the next of kin which is you. But before you can inherit the house you have to pay the duty to the Spanish government which you are in no position to pay. If you don't pay, they will start charging you interest and keep charging you until all of the equity is gone. What I suggest we do is that once your mother has had the operation, we fly her back to Spain to change the house into my name and once I inherit the house I will sell it and give you your share of the money". This conversation genuinely happened within an hour of me finding out that my mother was dying of a terminal brain tumour. I was having a conversation but I didn't believe I was having it because these kinds of things didn't happen in the real world. I had only one response "I don't care about the money Derick, just take care of my mum."

Still reeling from the totally inappropriate conversation I returned to the main room and I tried to remain as upbeat as possible, that is the family philosophy during times of crisis. After all, when you have just received news like that the last thing you need is people crying and throwing themselves to the floor, wrapping their arms around your ankles and screaming "please don't leave me". We spoke, as everyone does at times like these, of what we could do to make the situation better. The doctors had said that they wanted to do a major operation. They would cut open the skull and then go right to the heart of the brain and remove as much of the tumour as possible. The difficulty would be that you can't just take away the tumour and leave the rest of the brain fully intact. The tumour had grown in her brain and the more of it you took away the more of the brain you take away also. Even as I write it down the prospect is horrifying.

I remember an episode of Farscape where the hero had the bad guy living in one of the memories in his head. The only way to get rid of the bad guy was to get rid of the memory. Problem is they didn't know which one it was. So while he was awake, the doctor would describe to him one of his memories and based on how important it was to him, he would choose whether they should remove it, or he should keep it and hope that It wasn't the one that the bad guy lived in. It has stuck with me because I found the concept so frightening. Volunteering to have bits of your brain removed in the hope that it would make you better but knowing that at the same time it would also make you worse. It doesn't just sound frightening, it's fucking terrifying. What a choice. And it was a choice. She could refuse the operation and just go for chemotherapy and radiotherapy. This might hold the tumour at bay for a while but it would be nowhere as effective as the operation. Or nothing at all. Then the cancer would grow quickly and she would degenerate rapidly. One or the other, or both, or neither, ultimately it was up to Mum.

Thing is it's not really a choice. Some people believe that when faced with this range of options that they would actually say no. After all, these treatments are nasty. Lisa had an uncle once who was treated in the early days of chemotherapy. He was sick at home one day and his vomit melted through the floorboards. This is supposed to be medicine, not a scene from alien. You might think that you would choose to spend your last days without being radioactive. To top it all they had a cruise booked in January which was only just over two months away. If Mum refused the surgery she could still take the cruise but I can tell you now that if you were in Mum's position you would take the treatments. Everybody does and the reason for this is that life is precious. Just one more day, just one more sunrise, one more song. You would take the treatments. That and the fact that doctors will always give you a best case scenario. The surgeon who Mum had spoken to said that every person is different, some only live a while longer while others have gone on for another five years and you may actually go on for a lot longer than that. There are new drugs coming on to the market all of the time. That's what they say, five years, possibly more, doesn't sound so bad. I fucking hate them for that.

I once saw this natural history programme about spiders and in it there was this creature called a spider-wasp. This wasp lands on the back of a live spider and lays an egg there before flying away. When the wasp lave hatches it burrows into the back of the spider and eats it as its first fresh meal. All the time in-between the spider knows that the egg is there on its back but there is nothing that it can do about it. I think that cancer is like that, you know you have it, you know that it is going to kill you and you can do nothing about it. How can you carry on with such knowledge without going crazy? Yet people do. Every day.

A date for the operation was set and Mum had the top surgeon, he was a mister. I've never understood that. Why spend five years going through medical school so people will call you doctor and then another five years specialising in the subject so people can call you mister again? You sound just like any other man on the street. If that was me I would want a name better than doctor, like genius, or god. Derick's daughters had been told the news. I would like to hope that when they recognised the full gravity of the situation that they felt like a right couple of Charlie's but I doubt it. They both dropped everything and booked very expensive last minute flights so that they could be here to lend their support. I could kid myself that they were coming over to support my Mum but the real reason they were flying in was to make sure that their father was okay. The prospect of their presence actually made the situation worse. I would still be needed, lifts to London etc and I wanted to be around as much as possible. I had a word with my Dad who on hearing the news had agreed to help out me out financially. Things had been difficult for a long time. I used to work for my father before I went out my own and in the beginning the business was flying. Instead of working for him, handing over the take and getting wages I now ran my own business and bought from my father wholesale. Then things started to get tough and I would take the stock on tic but when I came to paying for it I couldn't because I had used the money to pay bills. I started to slip further and further behind, or more specifically father and father behind, which put pressure on our relationship. Any usual wholesaler would have just stopped supplying me and written the debt off but if he were to stop supplying me he would cut of the life line to his only son. I put him in a very difficult position and I don't like myself for that. I had told Dad of Mum's illness and he wanted to help in any way that he possibly could. Although he couldn't actually do much himself he said that he was prepared to give me whatever it took financially and so allow me to do whatever was necessary. This was good because it gave me the resource that I needed the most, time. I needed time to spend with Mum and being self-employed if you don't work you don't eat.

On the day of the operation I drove Mum and Derick to Queens Square. Fortunately, I know London very well because I spent eighteen months on 'the knowledge'. For those of you who don't know what that is, 'the knowledge' is the test that you have to pass if you want to become a black cab driver in London and it's really, really hard. Well not hard as such, just very, very long. First of all, you have to learn every single street name in the whole of London which is classified as a six-mile radius from King Charles's island,

41

the roundabout just south of the National Gallery. In addition to this you also have to learn all of the 'points of interests' within that radius. A point of interest can be anything from a hotel; to a restaurant; to a swimming pool; to an old Russian tank on some obscure housing estate that has been painted pink. There are twenty-five thousand streets in London and there are over thirty thousand landmarks to learn. Once you have got all of that sorted, you also have to know the shortest route between them all.

If you are ever in London, you can see the knowledge boys. Would be cab drivers flying around on mopeds with a Perspex windshield and a piece of paper attached with bull dog clips. It takes three years to do the knowledge if you study it full time. I was doing it part time. Furthermore, I didn't have a scooter so I had elected to do it on a push bike and then when this was taking too long I took to getting up at four in the morning and doing my 'runs' in a truck. It soon became clear, as time went on that I would run out of money before I could obtain my green badge and so I went on to a new venture but I still retain some of the things that I learnt and I certainly knew where Queens Square was. It is on the second run you have to study, round the corner from Great Ormond Street.

I drove Mum and Derick to the hospital. We all went in to meet the surgeon who was a handsome middle aged man with good hair and a posh accent. He told me he would take good care of Mum and that for a while after the operation she would be confused and muddled as her brain tries to recreate the neural pathways that had once existed. Work would be needed for her to properly regain all of old abilities and it may be a slow process but slowly she would return to her former self. Derick was going to stay in London with Mum. He had booked into a hotel around the corner and he would also be able to stay with Mum as she had her own room and there was a big reclining chair next to the bed. Good old BUPA. I would still be working on the markets but because I traded in London I could arrange for someone to take care of the stall and so I could jump on a tube and visit Mum every day. I gave Mum a hug and kiss, wished her good luck and told her that I would be up straight after the operation.

I never properly saw my Mum again.

Ch.6 Meet the Pirozzoli's

I went to see Mum the day after the operation and she had
changed. Funny that when you bear in mind that they had just
cut a great big chunk from out of the middle of her brain.
Derick was with her in the comfy chair next to the bed
holding her hand.

"How's it going mum?" I said

"Gehherrr ,   yeah." Was the reply.

I don't know what I expected. Yes I do, I expected her to be
fine. As I said earlier I'm the kind of guy who thinks you go
into hospital to get better. I am an idiot. In my defence, I had
also bought in to what the surgeon had told me. 'A bit
disorientated at first but with work she would become more
like her former self.' This wasn't disorientation, they had
turned my mother into a dribbling Muppet. I may be an idiot
but I am also a realist and so I quickly concluded that she had
just had major brain surgery and that to expect her to get out
Boggle or start on cryptic crosswords was a bit unrealistic
right now. I checked the wound on her head and while being
a reasonably sized scar they had managed avoid shaving off
too much of her hair. The importance of this is not to be
underestimated.

There are many parts to illness. Primarily there is pain. This is the worst bit. To live in pain is debilitating, tiring and most off all can change your perception of the world around you and how you are perceived by the world. If you are in pain you become snappy and short tempered and people start to think that you are nasty when in fact, you are just in pain. Remember whinging Wyne. My Grandma was a lovely woman, she wasn't nasty, she was just in pain. Oh if anyone thinks that they would just ignore the pain and carry on as if it wasn't there, you can't, its pain.

Next is the actual disability. Not being able to do things that you did before. This is tedious, frustrating and in some case's impractical. The result is that you now have to rely on other people either partly or fully to do things for you, which makes you feel wretched because of your own dependency. It's like being a child again but worse because when you were a child you couldn't do things because you didn't know how, you hadn't learned yet. Now you can't do things that you had previously been able to do. Things that you know how to do but that you are now unable to do. Losing a skill is worse than never having one in the first place. You take to constantly apologising for something which is not your fault.

Thirdly but also importantly there is appearance. Our place in the world and how we are accepted and perceived is through our appearance. We express our personalities through the clothes we wear and strangers will quickly assess us on what they see. Appearance is particularly important for women. I'm not saying that that's right, it's just the way it is.

So with that in mind I was pleased that they had managed to keep most of Mum's hair and that she had her makeup. A small leather bag the size of a shoebox containing a range of beauty products which cost more than I paid for my car. You see my point?

The whole scenario was a bit strange if I am honest. To walk in to Mum and Derick in a hospital room together. Strangely I felt a little out of place. She was my Mum and he was just a boyfriend but they had built a life together over the last decade and it was one that I had had little to do with. I may be blood but he was the one that she had chosen to spend her life with. If I had to choose between my wife and my family, I would choose my wife without hesitation so as far as I was concerned I had no more right to be in that room than he had. And it was Derick who was putting in all of the work. He was the one that had got the hotel room that he didn't use because he would sleep in the chair next to Mum all night, not me. I felt a little guilty and the reason that I felt guilty is that I didn't actually want to do it. Being in hospitals is unsettling, clinical and I'm sorry to say it boring. Sitting there watching the crap that they show on daytime TV, wishing away the day because at least at night time you can sleep and when you wake up you will be one day closer to getting out. In all fairness I still had to go to work and I had a family of my own to look after but this was my mother's hour of need. What do you think you would you do if your Mum had to go through a life changing operation? I wonder if what you think you would do and what would actually happen are the same thing?

There is also more to it than that. I believe that everyone has their own idea of hospitals and how hospital visiting should work. I think that you go into hospital to get better and a result of this you want to be left alone. Sure it's nice to get visitors from time to time, maybe for about twenty minutes or half an hour just so you know that the world outside has not forgotten you and that people still care. After that it would be nice if they would go. If you could just leave the grapes and magazines on the side I can go back to dozing and watching repeats of Top Gear. I've never been a great one for small talk at the best of times let alone when I am feeling wretched. In Spain they have a different approach. The nurses are just there for the medical things. The family is the one that tends to you, feeds you, washes you and changes your bed. They are there for a large amount of the time helping you though your recovery. Sounds like hell. Mum, like me, was used to the English system of hospitals. Pity that because it was about to get a lot worse. On the third time I came to visit Mum the rest of the clan had arrived. The double BUPA room was now Inhabited by Mum, Derick, Jane and Linda, Derick's daughters.

Now we had met very little and although it had never openly been said but we never really got on and there are a few reasons why. Derick had already gone through two wives. The first one, their mother committed suicide. She suffered from depression and Derick himself said that he'd not been a good husband. He was drinking at the time and although we never actually got to the bottom of it I believe that his first wife's suicide was one of the main reasons for him giving up the sauce. The other reason that may have led

47

to his first wife's suicide was because Derick was fraternising with wife number two Jill. This is the reason that the bar was called Derick and Jill's, although Mum had done a reasonable job of peeling Jill's name from the blue and white stripe tarpaulins that hung outside of the bar. The second marriage had been a tempestuous affair. Wife number two who was a drunk, made his life hell and after doing so, left him for another woman. Enter Mum who also liked a drink, could also be very opinionated especially with a drink and who was related to me.

There was also the 'Mum merry go round' which went something like this. Mum would return to England, come round for dinner, have too much to drink and then start a conversation with "I know I shouldn't say this but" and that's when you knew that you are in trouble because she would then go on to say something forthright, rude and wrong, normally concerning Lisa. As the real man I am I would turn round to my Mum and say how dare you talk to my wife like that. No I wouldn't. I would make some half-hearted effort to sweep the comment under the table and hope that it would all go away, which it never did. This then meant that I would then have to call Mum in the morning to let her know that she could not behave in this way. This conversation started with her saying "what have I done now". I would explain, badly because I am shit in arguments and Mum would go away behaving like a wounded animal despite being the one who had caused all of the grief in the first place. And although I don't know it for a fact, I would bet my house that she would be straight on the phone telling all concerned how we had been mean to her. Therefore, in their eyes we were the unreasonable family in England who didn't take proper care of their mother. Joke is, if I had to suffer Mums uncalled for comments I am sure that they did too and to make matters worse they are tee-total. I believe her comments would have gone down great in their household, over a family meal with Mum on her second bottle of chardonnay telling a sober audience where they are going wrong in their lives. You might think that after seeing Mum in full swing, they might have been a little more sympathetic. In my experience however empathy is something sorely lacking in most people and the way they see the world is different for others as it is for themselves. People have funny mirrors.

I have a theory on giving people advice. That is kind of my catchphrase, I have a theory on everything. Never give anybody advice unless they specifically ask for it. When someone comes to you and spills their heart out about something that is going wrong in their lives, they are not looking for you to provide a solution. You should listen, but say nothing. Unless they actually say to you "what would you do?" or "what do you think I should do?" then tell them. They asked. If they don't ask keep your mouth shut, they just want someone to talk to. There is nothing more irritating than advice givers. For example, take a phrase that I am sure that we have all said at least once in our lives: 'What you need to do is break up with them.' If you do use this phrase what you are probably failing to spot is that things might be hard for your friend at the moment but the person who you are talking to does actually love their partner and doesn't actually want the relationship to end. In my experience taking on someone else's partner, no matter how badly they are behaving ends badly for one person, you. Then there's the: 'what I would do is break up with them'. No you wouldn't. If you felt the way they do, then you would do exactly what they are doing and if you don't feel the same way that they do, then how are you in any position to give any advice? While we are on the subject and this is the one that annoys me the most, most people don't give you the advice that is best for you, they give you the advice that is best for them. 'What you need to do is break up with them' translates to: 'If you break up with them then you might come out more on a Friday night and I'll have someone to go on holiday with'. When I was studying I had a friend called Paul who had three axioms: never ask for anything more than twice; never refuse anything more than three times and never take anyone else's advice. These are self-evident truths; you can live by them.

As a result of this I believe that on the first time we ever met the siblings it is fair to say that we were on somewhat of a back foot. To be honest it was a bit like being on a table at a wedding. You know when the bride and groom put complete strangers on a table together so that they have a chance to get to know each other before the evening. If you are planning a wedding and you are thinking of adopting this technique allow me to enlighten you, don't do it, it doesn't work. What you actually end up with is tables full of people who have absolutely nothing in common. This leads to awkward silences and the most banal small talk from groups of people who can't wait to get up and leave to be with their friends, who have also been randomly scattered throughout the room. What you should do is put all the people who know and like each other together, they will have a good time and probably more than a couple of drinks and then, when sufficiently lubricated, find strangers to talk to at the evening do. That's what we did and I can honestly say mine is the best wedding I have ever been to. You might think that of course it was, you were the star of the show but that aside I actually thought that it was really good. So me and the family were sitting in a Spanish restaurant with people who had already prejudged us and who had a very low opinion of us because by proxy, we were related to Mum and because of the stories they were told, by Mum.

Now don't get me wrong, everyone was perfectly convivial. I talked to Linda's husband about his pool cleaning business and he was a thoroughly nice guy, hen pecked and boring but still very nice. Terrible word nice. 'How was your dinner?' it was nice. 'What was the room like? 'nice'. 'I'm going to the panto', that's nice. The only time when Nice is a good word is when it is on the French Riviera with a pebble beach and has a McDonalds that sells beer. I also spoke to Linda. Linda is a large forthright, and opinionated lady. In their family Linda had become somewhat of a matriarch and it is easy to see why. For a start they were all stranger's in a strange land. Scots in Spain. In addition to this if Derick had been drinking and running with a new woman while her mother had taken to her bed with depression that kind of left Linda to run the house and take care of her younger sister. Some people have to grow up quick and that's not actually a good thing. So we went to the restaurant with an open mind to find a bunch of people who had never met us but still had very little time for us. You know how I knew? Their smile didn't reach their eyes. The right words came out of their mouths but there was no sincerity there. It's like bad acting. Bad actors do what good actors do you just don't believe them. To be perfectly honest I didn't care. Why would I? They lived fifteen hundred miles away and I might have to see them once a year if I was unlucky. The only one I cared about out of them was Mum. Except all that had changed now.

So back in the hospital room, which even as a double room in the BUPA ward was now beginning to feel quite crowded. Imagine the front room of the Royle Family and transport it to a room with two beds, light blue walls and a large bright window overlooking a car park. The Pirozzoli's were slouching around in clinical armchairs staring at the television and right in the middle of it all and somewhat out of place was my mother, semi reclined on a motorised bed looking quite helpless. To make matters worse the sisters kept fussing over Mum. "Would you like another cushion Vicky?", "Can you see the television alright Vicky?", "Would you like something to drink Vicky?" All this time I was getting angrier and angrier; could they not see they were aggravating her? I wondered if they knew that they were annoying her and were actually quite enjoying it. Mum was totally helpless. She was bed ridden, had no mobility and her speech had become more limited. She was totally dependent, yet she could totally understand the world around her. It was like she had locked in syndrome. Perhaps I am being unfair, perhaps they were genuinely trying to help. It just felt a bit like playground bullying.

Thing is, I know that they had little time for Mum. Perhaps I should have said something but what could I say. If

I challenged them, said "can you stop that, can't you see that you're getting on her nerves." the response would be "I only asked if she wanted a drink". It was then that Derick dropped another bombshell. He said "We've been trying to get your mother to practice her writing again, the surgeon said that this will help with the recovery". Fair enough, that's very commendable. He then went on to say, "We've got her practicing her signature". On the face of it this also seemed like a sensible thing to do and one that would aid Mum's recovery. "And your mother is having trouble remembering her bank codes". Okay now I have put two and two together and gone straight from 'that seems like a good idea' to 'what the fuck?' Literally, WHAT THE FUCK! Why is he asking her about bank codes? And so blatantly. She was only a couple of days out of the operation and they were already attempting to access her money. Mob handed, which increased the pressure on Mum. It would be easy for her to say no to Derick, she had plenty of practice at that, but to say no to him and both his daughters was an entirely different situation. I knew that vultures would travel a long way for find prey but I didn't realise that they would fly all the way from Spain.

Derick went on to say that Mum always dealt with the money and he just needed access to her accounts in order to pay for things like the hotel and the hire car. This wasn't true. Mum had her money and Derick had his and Mum had kept it this way for a reason. They both had bank accounts and besides the car was on a credit card. It is true that in our naivety none of us expected Mum to be in the state that she was in, I certainly didn't. I am also aware that finances would have to be discussed. What I suppose bothered me the most as usual, was the timing. My mother was two days out of a life altering operation and incredibly vulnerable and here were three people whose most prominent concern seemed to be how they could access her finances. They didn't see Mums brain tumour as a tragedy, they saw it as an opportunity.

Ch.7 The Invaders

I left the hospital with all of these thoughts running through my head. I already knew that something was up as a result of the surreal conversation that I had had with Derick in the hallway but now things had moved to another level. I sometimes liken life and thought to the computer program's that I used to write at school. At any stage in your life your brain is running various different programs. The main one is what you are actually doing but there are always many others running in the background. I call these subroutines and they go round and round on a never ending loop. For example:

10 I'm fed up with my job

20 I should go on the net and see what else is out there

30 Chances are there is nothing out there and there is little chance I would get another job anyway because of the amount of applicants so I'll just have to stay where I am

40 Goto 10

These are the kinds of thoughts that are always running in the background of your mind. Some subroutines only crop up from time to time, some are bigger than others and some you never rid of. If you ever silence one by achieving the main objective, say by actually getting another job then all that happens is another one comes along to replace it. 'Now I've got a better job I can get a better flat'. You get the picture. Subroutines run all of the time like a high pitched whistle in the back of your mind, and they make you tired. Since I had found out about Mum's terminal illness the question of what was going to happen to her had been humming away in the back of my head. Now the subroutine had a subroutine of its own and it had a whistle louder than a steam train. Was her boyfriend and his family actually trying to take my mother's money?

Mum's time in hospital was coming to an end and it was clear that she couldn't go back to Bellows Mill. In her current condition she would need a high level of care, more than Derick would be able provide on his own. I had spoken to mister doctor and it had been decided that Mum would undergo a course of chemotherapy and radiotherapy over the next six months. This would hopefully shrink the cancer and restore Mum to something much more like her normal self. The cancer would never ever go but the aim of the treatment was to get it under control so that Mum could go back to a normal life again. On the day of her discharge I drove the mini up Queens to bring them back. The sisters gave us a hand with the luggage and out of politeness I asked them if they wanted to come back. They refused and as I watched them wander off through the immaculate garden opposite the hospital I thought there was a good chance that we would never meet again. A position that I'm sure suited both sides perfectly.

Once Derick and a poorly worse-for-wear Mum were safely ensconced in the family car I set off on the familiar journey from London to Eaton Bray. They couldn't go back to the Mill so of course they would have to come and stay with us, which made me happy. Mum would be in my home where she could be properly taken care of. Lisa keeps a lovely home. It is clean, it smells of scented candles and the food is good. I know it's my house but it is a lovely place to be. When Molly was growing up every time I walked in from work there would be some kid or other who had come back from the village skater park and was currently loitering around the kitchen eating our food. I didn't mind, to be honest it was quite flattering that they wanted to spend time there. Having Mum and Derick at home was also good because it meant no more trips to the hospital, going to hospital is a nause. Once you have to get there you have to find somewhere to park. I have never understood why you have a hospital that can hold, say, a thousand patients so they make available forty parking spaces. Then allocate thirty of them for staff. It's like some form of musical chairs. 'Should I wait here and hope that one becomes available or should I just go round and round in circles and hope for a miracle'. And you've got no chance of leaving it on any street within a two-mile radius because it has all been made 'residents parking only 'which is totally understandable as it means that now local people can actually park near their own home. You find yourself looking at wasteland or the pavement outside of shops thinking 'maybe I could leave it here, but what if I come out and the cars been clamped?' I don't believe that all hospitals are like this, just the ones that I seem to go to.

Then once you are in there is the familiar loiter around a bed before you can go home again. Obviously they are happy to see you and you are happy to see them but after the initial five minutes the rest of the visit descends into half an hour of banal conversation before you can go and leave the patient to do what they are supposed to be doing, rest and getting on with getting better. I believe than no one wants to be there and everyone is happy to leave but this is not the main reason that Mum and Derick coming home made me happy. When you have a loved one in hospital you just want to get them home. Even if this is a totally stupid thing to do. Even if you know that bringing them out will definitely kill them you want to put them in a wheelchair and then run down the corridors (in my mind I am being chased by doctors, white coats flapping behind them), pile them into a car and pull off, tyres screeching. Just so that you can get them home and give them a cup of tea in front of a warm fire and the telly and then tuck them up in bed because then everything would be alright. I felt like that. When we got back Lisa had prepared the main bedroom where they would be staying with fresh bedding and flowers and I was happy.

For the next few days we entered the twilight zone. When strangers move into your house the whole situation becomes somewhat strange. You get up in the morning and there is someone sitting at your table drinking coffee you think 'what are you doing here?' You start eating meals at different times. You can no longer get out of the bath and walk around naked into the bedroom to put your pyjamas on. It is like an invasion. An invasion that would go on for six months and it became clear very quickly that it was not going to work. This may seem a little harsh with Mum's condition but you have to bear in mind that Mum never came to stay with me even for a week because we would kill each other. The fact that she was now ill didn't change the way that we worked and now we were looking at six months which was somewhat unimaginable. If six months was insurmountable to me think what that would mean for Lisa. I had the refuge of work. For twelve hours a day I could escape to what would now be the relative peace and quiet of London street markets. And while Derick did tend to take Mum out during the day Lisa still had the full guest house regime. Combined with the fact that their relationship was tempestuous at the best of times meant that this was going to be a big ask.

It was my Dad who came up with the solution. Down the road at Bellows Mill, in addition to the small holiday lets, they also had holiday cottages. Proper self-contained living accommodation. We would move Mum and Derick in there. They would have their own front door just like they had back in Spain. There were enough of the family around to constantly pop in to make sure that they were okay and if there was anything they needed and we would sort out a car so they were free to go and do whatever they wanted. We would have Mum and Derick around for meals and evenings, we could even have Christmas together which was something that we had only done once in the previous ten years. They had always used the excuse that they had to run the bar but the real reason was that Derick wanted to be with his family and Mum had never stood up to him on that one. They would get a place of their own. Great, everybody wins. Dad would foot the bill. Heaven knows I couldn't. Dad was still fond of

Mum and had made the offer gladly. He had traded Mum for a younger model and although he would never admit it he carried guilt as a result. Now here was a chance to atone for his sins. Best of all he could buy his way out of it. No real contrition required, just an open cheque book and make things right. I have no idea what Beverley, the younger model thought of all this but she probably got little say in the matter. I know that early on in their relationship she tried to put the knife in with Dad as far as my Mum was concerned and got very short shrift. The reply to her attacks was "what's she ever done to you?" Beverley may have ultimately got my Dad but his fondness for my Mum never diminished.

As far as affairs are concerned I have a theory on this. Don't have them. Actually there is more to it than that, when you get married make sure that you marry the right person, it's not that tricky. The most important thing to remember is that you are choosing someone to spend the rest of your life with. I know that this sounds obvious but I genuinely believe that some people don't think about what is going to happen past the stag do, let alone the wedding. "I'll get married, that way I can have a two-week holiday in Benidorm with my mates". What you need to do is find someone who you think is beautiful, someone who treats you well and you get on really well with, like a best friend. Someone who you never run out of conversation with who supports you and wants what you want. Once you have found them marry them and be happy together. Think of it this way, if you had to buy a shirt and you were going to wear that shirt every day for the rest of your life you wouldn't get it from Primark. If you have any sense you would go to Savile Row and get a tailor made shirt, one that fits you perfectly. It may be expensive but you are going to wear it every day for the rest of your life. You wouldn't buy one that is likely to go out of fashion, one that doesn't suit you or that you would get bored with. You would buy a fine shirt. A quality shirt. A shirt that is totally right for you. I work on exactly the same principle with tattoos. If you are going to get a tattoo, then firstly make sure that what you are about to put on your body is something that you will be happy with for ever because that is how long it will be there. Then spend a lot of time and money making sure that you get what you want, it's that straight forward. That's why I haven't got a tattoo.

Don't pick a woman who gives you grief before you start as it's only going to get worse. I know that bad people are dangerous and exciting at first but ultimately that wears off and you just end up married to a bastard. Not a good move. Now I'm not saying pick someone who is reliable and dull, you still have to fancy them. Working out the right one was easy for me because I got struck by lightning but if that doesn't happen there is another way of telling. Ask yourself this question: 'when you see them, do they make your bum go tight?' As a bloke you may think it's enough if you rise to the occasion but let's face it as a young man this is hardly a litmus test. Once you have found the right woman marry her. Don't piss about stringing her along while keeping one eye out just in case something better comes along, women know what you are doing and they don't like it. If you are not careful you may lose the best thing that you ever had. If you like it put a ring on it. She may tell you that she is not interested in marriage. She's lying. She grew up watching

Disney princesses in huge dresses who get whisked off to a castle by a white knight on a strong horse to live happily ever after, can you blame her. She may also tell you that she doesn't want children. Chances are that this is a lie too. It's like you telling her that you don't want sex or you are not interested in porn. In all fairness they may also be lying to themselves and you can't blame them for that, it is the woman's prerogative to change her mind. And none of this I don't believe in marriage we are happy just the way we are nonsense, make a decision, show your colours and act. Otherwise you are just driftwood.

Once you are married be a good and faithful husband, you have to, you made a contract. I'm not a religious man, in fact I am an atheist. I would have been an agnostic but I'm sure that god hates agnostic's more than atheists so I chose the former. I may not believe in god, at least not in the conventional way, but I got married in a church. For some reason getting married in church felt like it gave our marriage more gravity, made it proper. Now if you get married in a church as well as having a contract with the state you also have one with god and I've read about what he is capable of. There's this book about him, it's called the bible. In it he: floods the earth, reigns down fire and brimstone upon a city and turns people to salt. Not only can he do anything but he can also see anything and knows everything so it's not even like you can get away with it by wearing a disguise and using a false name. And you've just entered into a contract with him. If you thought that borrowing money from the mafia was a scary thing to do, trust me, they've got nothing on god. He's one serious guy. Also I'm pretty sure that it says both in the book: 'thou shalt not commit adultery' and in the contract: 'forsaking all others'. There it is in black and white, you are not allowed to fuck other people. So don't do it.

That said if you do have a moment of weakness then you must never tell anyone. That is your punishment. For that one night of passion you must carry the knowledge around with you for the rest of your life. It will forever be a weight upon your shoulders, that is your penance for what you have done. If you confess to your partner and ask them to forgive you all you are doing is taking the mill-stone from around your neck and placing it around theirs. Once you confess you will instantly feel relieved but they will then know that you betrayed them and that's a really shitty thing to do. You fucked up, you carry it. In all fairness to my Dad, he did. I'm sure that he had affairs before but he had never told my Mum and he always returned to her. I am sure that it would have been the same scenario this time if my step-Mum hadn't planted the pants in the laundry bin. She says that she didn't but she did. You don't accidentally make a mistake like that. She set out to get my Dad by any means necessary and that's not right. If all is fair in love and war, then why do we have the Ottawa treaty and the Geneva Convention?

Oh and if despite your best intentions it turns out that you made a mistake and married the wrong person and the two of you are no longer in love which can happen then leave. Don't start behaving like you are single or stay together for the sake of the kids because that never works. Admit it and settle your affairs with dignity and then move on. Accidents happen and you have the rest of your life to try again. My parents settled their affairs with dignity. Mum said what's the point of having a big fight about it? All that would happen is they would take what money they had and divide it equally between the solicitors. As a result, my Mum and Dad were still friends. As time had gone by Mum and Derick and Dad and Beverley actually got together socially and even went out for dinner together. I don't applaud this, it's just weird. You know when people break up but say 'let's still be friends'. No you can't be friends, you can never be friends with someone that you once loved. You can see each other; you may even get on well but you can never be just friends. Not anymore. Mum and Dad were more than friends. I think that despite what he had done she still loved him and if she could she would have taken him back and I think that he also still had some love for her. Certainly enough love to do whatever was necessary to help with her illness. We arranged for them to move into the mill. Everything was going to be okay. That's when things really started to turn to shit.

Ch. 8 People can get it so wrong

It was the next day when I returned from work that it happened. We had established a kind of working routine at home. I would go to work and Derick would take Mum out for the day. At around five we would all convene around the dining room table where we would discuss our days before having dinner. We would eat, watch TV and then go to bed. Just like in any other house. On this particular night I walked into my house in the twilight zone again, all was the same and everything was different. Derick had decided that he wanted to return to Spain. His life was in Spain. His business, his children and grandchildren were in Spain. He didn't want to stay with Mum and look after her. Instead he wanted to leave Mum with us while she underwent the two months of chemotherapy treatment. Then came the kick. Before Mum started her treatment Derick wanted to take her back to Spain for a couple of days, enough time for the house to be transferred into his name because if they left it too late then there was the possibility that she would not be in a well enough state to do the relevant paper work.

You couldn't make it up.

I couldn't believe I was hearing it and more to the point I couldn't believe that he was actually saying these words out loud right in front of my mother. She sat there like an enormous teddy bear that nobody wanted. Clearly I had something to say on the matter. I wasn't nasty. I find that often nasty gets you nowhere. Start from a reasonable point of view that way if the conversation turns sour you always have nasty to fall back on. I just explained to him that he couldn't go back to Spain. As her full time partner of the last ten years' Mum would need him here while she underwent the treatment. After a lot of persuading Derick being the soft individual that he was agreed that he was needed and that he would have to stay. Then he said "I'll just fly back for a couple of days to get some clothes and things in order then I'll come back." Mum was in tears. "No" she said, "you won't come back." He said that he would but we all knew that that was a lie. If he went away then that would be it, I doubted whether he would ever see Mum again. In the middle of it all was my Mum who after a life changing operation was being made to feel that now she was damaged nobody wanted her any more, like her life had been so worthless in her time of need there was no one who would come to her aid. Then she said it. "I've got money." With those three words she broke my heart.

Like it was all about money. I wish it was, it would have made the whole thing so much simpler. Sometimes you can get it so wrong. There are certain things people say all of the time that are the wrong way around. I never understood why people say you can't have your cake and eat it. Yes you can. You buy a cake from the shop so you have a cake and then you eat it. That's how it works. No the phrase should be you can't eat your cake and still have it. The same is true for the best things in life are free. This makes you think of trees and flowers and stuff. Whoop de do. Actually it's not about trees and flowers at all, lovely though they all may be. It's about family and friends, it's about love. The phrase should be the best things in life are the ones you can't buy. You can't buy love. Everybody tells me so. You can't buy laughter with friends and you can't buy family but they are not free, not by a long chalk. You have to earn them. You earn trust. You earn respect. Having a family requires time and effort and sacrifice and this never ends. You can't buy it with money but it is certainly not free. Here I was trying to take care of mine.

My family is my wife and daughter. My Mum had decided to move to Spain and get a new family and when she came home she tended to cause grief and have little to do with her only grandchild, Molly, much to incredulity of my wife. However my Mum, despite her actions is still also my family and from a purely selfish point of view I wanted her here where I could help her and see her. I would have had her come to stay with us. I wanted her to stay with us but I knew that the stress that it would have put us under would have caused a rift so great that it could ultimately end up in the breakdown of my marriage and that is a risk that I was not prepared to take. And there was another factor. When you bring ill health into a house it affects the houses soul. The shadow of cancer brings with it a smell. It is the smell of drugs and nappies. It is the smell of death. Up until this point Molly's life had been charmed. She lived life as a happy sheltered individual and she was maturing into a strong beautiful young woman and I could let nothing compromise that.

There is a school of thought out there that says that children should be exposed to the horrors of the world around them. They should be informed of exactly what is going on and not sheltered. They need to know the truth, to know the world as it actually is. This way they will grow up quickly and be prepared for what life has in store for them. This is the biggest load of bollocks that I ever heard. Childhood innocence is the most precious thing and it should be protected at all cost. I intended to protect my daughter's. If Mum was to enter the house it would affect Molly perception of the world forever. Ask me to choose between my mother and my child, it's not a decision that I would need a lot of time to make. Despite being an easy decision my choice not to take care of my mother personally is still one that I beat myself up about nearly every day. I shouldn't though because it wasn't even an issue. We had the solution. Mum and Derick would get their own place and we would all pitch in. He just had to agree to stay and he had. He tended to do that, it's a technique.

I learned a long time ago that there is no point trying to change some one's beliefs with an argument. You can test this if you like next time you end up in a debate. I have found that the more you try to convince someone that they are wrong the more they dig their heels in and believe that they are right. You're better off just pretending to agree with them while keeping your own opinions. It's quicker, there is less fuss and the results the same. Unfortunately, Derick knew this too. What he would do was agree with you to let you believe that he would do one thing and then go off and do something completely different. The man took moving the goal posts to a premier league level. Nevertheless he had been backed into a corner and so Derick telephoned Linda to inform her that he would be staying in England with Vicky to help her with her recovery, news that went down like a cup of cold sick. Then Linda asked to speak to me.

Linda went straight for the jugular. Shouting, she informed me that her dad should not stay in England as he had a heart condition. I pointed out that my mother was dying of a terminal brain tumour which kind of trumped her ace lead. Then Linda told me what a terrible son I was because I was not prepared to look after my mother and if her father was sick she would look after him. I pointed out that I was prepared to look after my mother but the fact that her dad who had been her life partner for last decade thought it was okay to fuck off back to Spain in her time of need was totally unacceptable. There was some swearing and the conversation ended. At the end of the day she could say what she liked, I had them both here with me and they weren't going anywhere, that was that. Two minutes later the phone rang again and it was Jane, the other sister. It was a similar conversation to the first one only shorter and with less swearing. Derick talked to his daughters and explained to them that he was going to stay and look after Vicky, he was needed here and it was the right thing to do.

Three days later I came home to find Mum and Derick sitting at the dining room table. They were going back to Spain.

Derick and Mum had spent the last three days visiting her friends with him painting a picture of how unhappy they would be here and how they would be so much better off in Spain. Their house there would not be viable for them to stay in because it was a three story townhouse and Mum would have difficulty climbing the stairs. Instead they would move in with Linda. They could have the main bedroom and Linda would convert the adjoining room into an en-suite bathroom. Mum would pay. They had also spent the last three days visiting Lloyd's Bank and the Halifax so that Mum could give Derick access to her accounts. He never had any intention of staying; the whole thing had just been a smoke screen; he was just buying time. Time enough to access all of her assets and now that he had that he was in a position to leave. The only thing is that he couldn't go without Mum. I think that if he could've he would've but no such luck. Perhaps it was for the best.

Mums treatment was available in Spain. The Spanish doctors would take over where the English ones had left off and the standard of Spanish healthcare is at least as good as it is here. Also Mum would be around her friends and in familiar surroundings, much as I still think of her home being England she was an ex-pat, Spain was her home. If they stayed in England they would just sit in the holiday cottage between treatments watching television. It would be no life. With this in mind I of course reacted to this news in my normal controlled manner. No I didn't. I shouted at Derick saying that I couldn't believe that he was even contemplating this and that they were being ridiculous, rounded up Lisa and Molly and went to the pub. I didn't know what else to do. Sometimes you just have to get out. I had wanted to keep my Mum in England but now she was returning to the Costa del Sol and there was nothing that I could do about it but be angry. Me, Lisa and Molly sat in the pub considering the situation and I came to terms with the new set up. At certain times in your life you are presented with a fait accompli. You might think that you have a choice at the beginning but the choice is never there. It is like the choice you have when a magician asks you to pick a card. You may think that you are free to choose but actually the card you choose was set before you even saw the deck. It's called a card force. It's not real magic it's a trick and that's how tricks work. I know, I used to be in the 'Luton Mystic Ring'. Not all of life is like that, I don't believe in fate I believe in free will and I feel compelled to say that. It just so happens that in this part of the game we had all made our moves and I had lost. I would acquiesce to their request. I didn't want to cause my Mum any more pain but it was a bitter pill to swallow.

With the future predetermined it was now just a question of logistics. Mum had just had a major brain operation so she could hardly just jump on a plane although it was really tempting. We live twenty minutes drive from Luton Airport. Even with luggage you can clear security and be sitting in Frankie and Benny's in just over an hour. Once on the plane Mum would be in Malaga airport, twenty minutes away for her home in just three hours. There was only one problem. Planes fly at thirty thousand feet and the fact that the increase in pressure could cause Mum's brain to explode. Okay that's a bit dramatic but there was the definite possibility that the flight may cause her serious problems. They could drive and stay at various hotels on the way down but this is a long process and I think they wanted to be home as soon as possible. Obviously their only concern here would have been for my mother's safety and had nothing to do with Derick's desire to change the name on the deed's from Coath to Pirozzoli. Obviously. A boat would take forever and so the only possibility was the train. Their plan was to get the Eurostar out of St Pancras to Paris. From there they could get a train to Barcelona and finally they could get a connecting train to Malaga where one of the family would be there to pick them up.

At the age of 21, I was what I fondly refer to as a student wanker. The name comes from a character in a Viz cartoon. During this time, me and three mates put a selection of our belongings in a rucksack and set off across Europe to discover its architecture and culture thanks to the courtesy of it's wonderful rail network. I say culture it was actually more of a massive European piss up; within twenty-four hours we were in Magaluf (it did involve a ferry). Having said that I did end up seeing some wonderful places such as Rome, Venice and Prague. I also drank a lot of beer and despite have more than two dozen condoms that my mate Gary had stolen from the warehouse he was working in, totally failed to get a shag. Europe's trains are wonderful, they are clean and efficient and if you're clever about it you can learn to sleep on the foot-wide luggage racks which means that people can't kick you as they walk down the corridors. Yes, Europe's trains are wonderful but not when you have just had major brain surgery and not when you're wearing a nappy.

Since the operation Mum had lost a lot of her mobility and control of her body. She could still walk but she was now much more unsteady on her pins and there was the possibility that at any moment her bowels would become the bowels of despair, hence the nappy. Before the operation Mum had trouble remembering the odd word, after the operation she was faced with the possibility that she might fall over at any moment and the chance that she might shit herself. Mister doctor told us that there would be consequences, that everyone reacts differently and that they wouldn't know how bad it was until they opened her up. I don't believe this. They know. They're experts for fuck sake, they see the same thing day in and day out and I bet a pound to a penny that the results are always the same. When you take your car into a garage they know roughly what's wrong with it and how far gone it is. I've seen them on the Antiques Roadshow. Someone brings in a piece and they can tell their Louis the XIV from a Ming and you think 'how do they know that?' Because they see it every day, that's how. I think surgeons know exactly the way it will go but each time they do it they hope that they might learn something or at least to get a little better at the operation. That's why a group of patients is called a practice, they are using us to practise on. Or perhaps they don't know and truly believe that they can remove enough of the cancer to leave the patient relatively unscathed but with a significantly increased life expectancy. No, I don't buy it.

I also have a reason why I shouldn't buy it. After Mum's operation, during the time that Mum and Derick were staying with us, when we still thought that she would be receiving her treatment in England, we took a trip up to see an oncologist. This trip was to the University College Hospital which is just off of the Euston Road. It is a large modern office block style of building, the kind that looks like it has been made of glass and steel. The central reception is a spacious atrium where a smartly dressed cross section of Londoners sit behind desks and in front of computers ready to direct you to the relevant part of the monolith. We were directed upstairs and after a relatively long wait in an equally modern waiting room we were ushered in to a small office where a smart well-spoken gentleman explained to my mother what treatments were in store for her. Once all had been said and the three of us had gotten up to leave I asked if I could have a word with him in private. I asked him the important question, the one I didn't want to ask in front of my Mum.

"How long has she got?"

"Fourteen months."

That was his reply, simple as that. No 'well it depends on the individual' or 'we simply don't know each case is different'. Fourteen months, that was it. What really rung true was that his answer was so precise. He didn't say 'around a year' or 'eighteen months' he said 'fourteen'. Why would you pick that as a number unless you knew it to be exactly right? Later I pulled Derick to one side and told him what the oncologist had told me. I explained that I didn't want to say anything in front of Mum because like the surgeon said once you put a number on something it becomes a self-fulfilling prophecy. By the time we sat down to dinner the following evening he had told her.

Still what is done is done. My mother was now a shadow of her former self but she had made the decision with her boyfriend that they would return to Spain, return home, and there was nothing I could do about it. We came back from the pub and I told them that I was not happy with their decision but if that is what they had decided to do I would respect their wishes. I would even help in any way I could. The train was due to leave early Monday morning so I booked a hotel for the night in Kings Cross and late Sunday morning I put the luggage in the boot of the Jeep, Lisa said her goodbyes in a 'perhaps it's for the best' way, Molly said goodbye to her grandma for what was most likely to be the last time she would ever see her, then me, Mum and Derick set off for London.

Conversation on the way up was pleasant which was strange when you bear in mind I was talking to the person who was practically kidnapping my Mum, but that is the way that life actually works. I remember watching the Jack Nicholson film 'About Schmidt'. It's a road movie in which Jack's character is travelling to give the father of the bride speech at his estranged daughter's wedding. He is unhappy with his daughter's choice of husband and throughout the film he is musing on what he will actually say when he is in front of the wedding congregation. The whole film is a build up to when he actually gets the chance to speak his mind and finally put the record straight. When it comes to him giving the father of the bride speech I readied myself for his eloquent blistering attack. It didn't come. Instead he gave a fairly average 'wishing you all the best in your future happiness' type of affair. It may not have been the vitriolic rant I was hoping for but I did think, 'that's right, that's how it actually happens'. People say things like: 'if I'd have been there I wouldn't have let him get away with it' or 'if it had been me I would have said this/hit him'. No you wouldn't. No one ever does. I've seen it. Oh and if your pissed off that I ruined the end of 'About Schmidt' for you it was out over fourteen years ago so I blame you for not watching it sooner. While we're on the subject Darth Vader is Luke Skywalkers dad and at the end of sixth sense Bruce Willis turns out to be a ghost.

St Pancras station is my favourite building in the entire world. The outside is a fantastically intricate piece of gothic architecture and the inside is a perfect juxtaposition of history and modernity. Inside there are two wonderful statues, one huge and one pertinent. The huge one is called 'the meeting place' and it is of a wartime couple reuniting. If someone tells you that they will meet you under the statue don't ask "how will I know where it is?" because this will just make them laugh. It's really, really big. However perhaps the better of the two is the smaller one. It is a statue of John Betjeman. Betjeman was an English poet, writer and all round eccentric. More than this though he was a lover of trains and in the sixties when they wanted to remodel St Pancras and make it more like the monstrosity that is Euston station he fought and fought to prevent it. He fought and petitioned so hard that he actually won and it is because of him that St Pancras still stands. If you are ever there go and find his statue with its scruffy collar and broken shoe lace. A man of integrity, not vanity. The station also has many bars and shops, it has a piano that anyone can play and a champagne bar that sits alongside a platform from where trains will take you to Paris. How romantic. Today was not romantic. Today my favourite building was taking away my Mum.

I really should have been angry but instead I felt strangely comforted. The three of us had lunch in the hotel bar that resides within the great station and all the time it just felt like a massive countdown. Like time spent on the morning of an exam. You just want to wish it away. After lunch I took them to their hotel room and that is where I said goodbye. Not in the grandness and majesty of the station but instead in the narrow hallway of a Novotel hotel room. On a grey carpet next to a Corby trouser press. I said that I would call her every Sunday morning just like I always did when she was in Spain. Then I cried, I tried not to and I tried my best to hide it but it was too much. Derick also cried. Mum didn't cry. She couldn't. She said "I want to cry but I just can't cry anymore." It was one of the side effects of the operation; it took some of her emotional feeling away. Then I left the room and walked quickly down the corridor, out of the hotel and back to the safety of my car. I drove home wondering if I would ever see my mother again.

Ch. 10 Sleeping with the enemy

Derick called me when they got back to Spain, I had asked
him to. I wanted to know that they had arrived safely and that
the journey had hopefully not been too painful for Mum. In
all honesty it wasn't the best. Derick is a little man and my
Mum had become even more of a substantial lady as time had
gone by. What with her lack of manoeuvrability and the fact
that they had luggage it was an arduous affair to say the least.
On top of this was the fact that Mum was now not properly in
contact with her bowels and toilets on trains are not the most
convenient. Still they made it and they had moved into
Linda's which is where I would now have to call them. This
was not the greatest news for me particularly as the last time
that had I spoken to Linda our conversation had consisted
largely of swearing.

The Sunday morning phone call now reached a new
level of awkwardness. I would call Linda who would answer
the phone in a chirpy manner, until she realised that it was me.
I would ask to talk to my mother. Linda would pass me over
without saying a word. I would then try to talk to Mum
although her vocabulary was still very limited and getting
sentences out was something of a challenge. Instead what
tended to happen is that rather than talk to Mum I would talk
at her. I would tell her about what was going on in England,
trying to focus on the better things like how Molly was getting
on in school and the funny things that had happened on the
market that week. Derick would then come on the phone to
tell me what was happening with Mum's treatment, which I

was grateful for and the changes that he had made to her personal finances, which I was not. At least he was up front about it. Actually I think the appropriate word is brazen. Finally, we would discuss me coming over to visit Mum. We would discuss it because apparently now was not a good time.

It was around this time that I came back into contact with my Mum's old friend Jude. Jude is a strong willed woman who is not afraid to speak her mind, which in the past probably helped her when it came to dealing with my Mum. You see when Mum gave me a hard time, which she often did, in order to get sympathy or just make me feel guilty, I would end up feeling wretched. When she tried this tack on Jude she would just say "oh shut up Vicky." Mum would laugh and that would be the end of that. This was also a trick that Lisa eventually employed and one that alas I never learned. Or perhaps it is that I am in the unique position that if I ever did tell my Mum to shut up then she would act even more hurt and I would end up feeling even more wretched.

Mum and Jude had been friends since Kents. They drifted apart for a while and then reconnected years later when they became the best of friends again. Good friends are like that. I remember one of my teachers from sixth form telling us that he had hooked up with his best friend of old who he had not seen for years and they sat in the pub with nothing to say to each other. All I can say to that is perhaps they weren't that good friends. I hadn't seen my old university friend Graham for twenty years when one day he turned up in the neighbourhood. He had brought the family down to see the Harry Potter experience at Watford and suggested that we meet up. We sat in the pub and didn't stop talking. Mum and Jude were like that. Particularly after the first bottle of Chablis.

Anyway Jude contacted me. She had been speaking to Mum on the phone prior to the operation and she was not happy about the way things were panning out. Jude was concerned that Mum was not being properly taken care of and that she was being press ganged into doing things financially that she didn't want to do. The fact that someone else shared my concerns was supportive because even when all the crazy is happening you still end up asking yourself the question 'would other people feel like this or is it just me?' I told Jude that I was keen on travelling to Spain to see my mother and Jude suggested that we went out together. Lisa had said that she would come with me but I didn't want to put her through that and besides she had to look after Moll so Jude's suggestion came as somewhat of a relief. I wasn't afraid to confront the enemy on my own but I must confess that it wasn't a prospect that I was looking forward to.

It was also a big sacrifice that Jude was making. Jude is, what I suppose you would call, a single grandmother. She had two children which she raised independently because her and her husband split up when they were young. They remained and still are good friends but Jude said that they started to drive each other mad and so decided that they were better off apart. Jude worked hard all her life. She raised her children, paid for her house and then when they were all grown up decided that life in Luton at Monarch Airlines was no longer what she want so she sold up and moved to

Cornwall for a better life. However, there was a fly in the ointment. Her daughter who up until this point had been relatively normal individual fell in with the wrong crowd, got pregnant and then soon after turned into the poster girl for the Jeremy Kyle show. Drinking, drugs and debauchery. In the middle of it all was a young innocent child and Jude couldn't stand idly by watching this happen so she took in the young cherub and the task of raising a child, again. A task that she thought that she was done with. All of this also came at great financial cost to Jude who is not a rich woman and if you take on a child it not only limits your ability to work but they can also be really expensive things to run. Still I know she has no regrets. She loves Lilly more than life itself and she would now have to leave the child and find the money for flights and accommodation so that she could accompany me to Spain. Jude is a good friend.

I set about trying to make dates with Derick as to when would be the best time to visit my mother. Up until this point Derick had always stated that it was important that I should come and see Mum as often as possible, that she would need my support and of course we both knew that there was only a finite amount of time left. In truth we all only have a finite amount of time left but your perception of this is radically altered as soon as someone puts a figure on it. However as soon as I started to try to make plans to go over to Spain things started to get difficult. The difficulty apparently lied in the fact that they were living with Linda. Obviously there was no way in hell that I was going to stay there and had every intention of getting a hotel or B and B from where I could visit Mum at a convenient place. I'm not stupid. I knew that tensions between our families were running high and I had no desire to make matters worse. I was still not happy with the way that things had panned out but practicalities must prevail. Derick was looking after Mum now and what would be the gain in making his job harder? Furthermore, any additional grief that I piled on would only cause Mum more worry. It was around this time that I decided that there was a bigger picture going on here and whatever decisions I took from this point onwards had to be based upon my Mum's welfare. This was clearly the right thing to do. If only I had properly thought it through.

Derick stated that perhaps it was not a good idea for me to fly over to see Mum at the moment as it would exasperate the current situation. Things were difficult over there with the sisters and living in Linda's house made it all very delicate so perhaps it would be better if Jude came on her own. So just to recap, after watching my mother being taken away from me by a bunch of people who seemed hell bent on stealing her money I am now being told that I am not allowed to visit. Any idea of what that does to your imagination? I spent days on the market where I wasn't really there because my mind was wandering off somewhere worrying about how my Mum was being treated? Surely there couldn't be any form of physical abuse? What about mental abuse? Was she just stuck in her bed all day long? Derick said that she was being well taken care of but then Derick said all sorts of things that he clearly didn't mean. No she had to be okay otherwise they wouldn't have invited Jude. Then one late Thursday night the phone call came.

Jude was on the line. She had just had a massive row with the sisters. Up until this point Jude had been in communication with them (Linda was talking to her) but on this particular evening thing's had gone sour. Linda would tell Jude that the visit was happening one way and then keep changing the plans. First Jude was to stay with them. Then it would be better if Jude could find somewhere to stay but that she could see Mum whenever she liked. Then it would be find somewhere to stay and we will arrange when it is convenient for you to see Vicky. Every time you agree to a new rule they would implement another. This is how they worked.

I have another friend called Phil and he is the most random person that I have ever met. We were all big drinkers at University and we came out with fairly large overdrafts. In truth we were the lucky ones. We studied at a time when your fees were paid and Stella was £1.12 a pint. Phil worked out that if he got a job in a warehouse working nights he could pay the whole thing back in nine months. Not only would he be earning but he would not be spending because he was not going out. He did it. He did nine straight months' work and didn't go out once. When he finally got his first pay packet clear of any overdraft do you know what he did? He bought venetian blinds for his bedroom. You would think that you would go out and celebrate, not Phil. He had a radio in his car with all of the five presets set to Radio 1. When I asked him why he said "I like Radio 1". He recently brought a new Mercedes but brought the left hand drive model because it reminded him of being on his holidays. What is the point of this? When Phil wanted to split up with a girl he never told her. He would just act in a more and more unreasonable manner and when they asked him "What's wrong?" he would say "Nothing". He would do this until they were eventually forced to split up with him. That way he didn't have to go through all of the grief of dumping them. For most people being dumped is unpleasant, for Phil it was just easier. This is what Linda did to Jude. She made the conditions of her visit more and more difficult until Jude was forced to say something and then she was told that she was not welcome. Now my Mum was stuck out in Spain totally isolated from her friends and family.

Ch11. The Windmills of my Mind

Not knowing what was going on in Spain turned my mind to the dark place. It led to the sort of irrational thoughts that appear when your imagination is free to wander out of control. What are they doing out there? I should go out there and bang on the door and demand to see my Mum? No, what if they didn't let me in. I should go out there with the heavy mob then they would have to let me in? No what I should do is go out there with the heavy mob, abduct Mum, bundle her into the back of a hire car and race to the airport where we could get her on a plane and fly her home to safety. She can't fly. Okay we will bundle her into the back of a hire car and race to the station and get her home on the train. What if they call the police and get the train stopped? We would be arrested and they would still have Mum. Okay we drive over there, get Mum into a car and we drive back to England staying in random hotels along the way. It would be difficult for Mum but ultimately I could get her to safety. All kinds of crazy starts to go through your mind. It's not pretty. Fear leads to anger, anger leads to hatred and hatred leads to the dark side, or at least, to the dark place.

Incidentally you know how sometimes there is something in your life that is not right. For example, your daughter is hanging around with a waste of space boyfriend who treats her badly or you are owed money by someone who isn't paying you despite the fact that they have just booked a family holiday to Disneyland? That's when during pub conversations the phrase appears "What you should do is send the boys in". What we are talking about here is taking the law into our own hands. Getting together with people you know to basically go round and frighten someone into doing something that they should be doing anyway. Problem is this doesn't happen in the real world. Even if you do know a group of lads who are big and relatively handy you just don't go round threatening people. In the real world, we have families and there is such a thing as a police force that will come and arrest you if you start arbitrarily harassing individuals. I used to watch the show and so I know that the A Team are difficult to find. In real life no one knows a group of hard men who would go in and sort the problem out for you. Except actually, I do.

When things were hard on the markets I tried to turn my hand to other professions. At first I was going to become a black cab driver so I started doing the knowledge. It proved that the cash would run out before I passed out so instead I took to doing removals. I had a truck and a rented warehouse and lifting things in and out of vans had been part of my job for a while now so it seemed like a natural progression.

A job came my way clearing out the rooms of a hotel in Buckingham Gate London. The hotel was being refurbished and a guy contacted me who had brought the hotels old furniture. The problem was that lorry taking the goods away was a forty footer and was too big to get to the back of the hotel from where the old furniture would have to be removed. He needed a smaller lorry and a crew of men to ferry the goods from the back of the hotel to the big lorry in the front. For three days me and four of Molly friends from the skater park moved furniture. I took time off from the market and financed what turned out to be a three-day job. I have never done business this way. You sell a pack of socks and someone gives you the money, simple. This time I invested what little money I had in what was a big job for me ready for a large pay-out at the end.

We finished the job and the guy told me to come to the showroom where they exhibit the furniture Monday to collect my money. Then he said not to come Monday as Monday was not good for him, instead come Tuesday. Then he said he could not do Tuesday so he would put the money in my bank. It didn't appear. I phoned the office and they said that it had been sent by Bacs payment and that it may take a week to come through. No one uses Bacs payments anymore. This is the twenty first century and we may not have flying cars but I have my bank on my telephone and I was now starting to get nervous, but I waited hopefully. It didn't happen. That's when I found out the guy was a con man. I went on the internet and googled him. He would employ small firms to do jobs for him and then not pay them. He would sell the furniture overseas and then not ship it and he would buy furniture on credit and then not pay. Then he would field any advances for payments for as long as he could until finally closing the company and all of the debts with it and then open another company with a virtually identical name and do the whole thing all over again. The man's name is Michael Whitchurch and he runs Anglia Wholesale in Peterborough. He is a complete cunt.

I was broken. It was the time of my Mum's 60th birthday and we were all supposed to be flying over to Spain to help her celebrate. She had even paid for the flights and as she paid she said "You won't let me down will you Peter, you will definitely come". The money from the job was going to pay for trip away and now it wasn't there. On the day of Mum's sixtieth birthday rather than joining her in Spain I was parked outside a yellow storage unit in East Finchley just off of the north circular. I rang Mum to wish her a happy birthday but it didn't go well. She told me that the time I rang was the time not long after the plane had landed and that she had hoped that I had found some way to make it out and surprise her. Like I needed help feeling worse that I already did and it was all Whitchurch's fault. Never steal if there is a direct victim but Mick didn't care about that. He blatantly ripped people off, in fact I think he was even proud of it, I think he thought that he was some kind of modern day Maverick. Worse still there was nothing that I could do. I knew how the guy operated, besides the removal business was in its infancy and it wasn't exactly kosher. I would just have to wipe my mouth and walk away but the whole thing did leave rather a bitter taste. It was about a week after this realisation that I was working Queens on the Thursday. Needless to say I wasn't exactly behaving like my usual happy out going self. My friend Donna who ran the flower stall opposite me asked me what the matter was, so I told her. Her response was simple: "My Dave won't stand for that".

Dave was her husband. By day he drove the lorry that delivered the bread to Frank's supermarket in the Crescent and by night he was head doorman at the Ocean club on Mare street opposite Hackney town hall. Dave is a man of morals. He is a very sensitive caring man who loves animals. He has dogs and parrots and for a while was a vegetarian. He hates confrontation, but he is not scared of it. He is also six foot four and about four-foot-wide with a bald head, teeth like a broken piano keyboard and a voice that makes James Earl Jones sound like Joe Pasquali. And Dave can handle himself. You don't fuck with Dave.

I first properly got to know Dave through my mate Ken. Ken in his infinite wisdom decided to sleep with the girlfriend of a kick boxing bouncer who found out about the liaison and paid Ken a visit. After having a quiet word with Ken behind the van and sweeping Ken' legs away so he wound up on the floor the bouncer left warning Ken that if he went near this girlfriend again next time he wouldn't be so lucky. Ken basically shit himself. He went into a flat spin about it, terrified that the guy would come back. I said that I would speak with Dave to see if there was anything that he could do to smooth the waters. Being a doorman I thought he might know the guy, or at least know someone who did. Maybe he could help to stem any further reprisals. Turns out that doormen are not telepathically linked and Dave had never heard of him. Dave's take on the situation was that Ken deserved everything that was coming to him for sleeping with someone else's girlfriend, like I said, he is a man of morals. However, in his expert opinion Ken had been given a warning and there was little chance that the guy would be back. After that me and Dave became friends. Not exactly close friends more the kind you nod to and can pass the time of day with. That was until the Whitchurch affair.

After Donna's response nothing happened for a couple of months. To be honest I wasn't surprised. No one ever does what they say they are going to do. I would just have to accept the fact that I had been turned over. That's the way it goes, life ain't fair and the world is mean. Then I got the phone call. It was Dave. He apologised for not getting in touch earlier but explained that he had been off work with a bad back brought on by lifting extremely heavy weights. He told me that he would be off to visit our friend Michael in the next few days. A couple of days later Dave accompanied by a six foot seven scouse bloke who apparently made Dave look small and another guy who was as wide as he was tall turned up at Anglia Wholesale. Unfortunately, Michael wasn't there so instead they escorted one of his employees into the car park where the conversation went like this:

"You can tell your boss that he has a week to pay and if he doesn't then we will be back". said Dave to Whitchurch's employee, dragging on a Benson.

"You do know who he is, you do know he's been to prison". replied the employee. This is in fact true. He has been to prison several times for fraud. In fact, he once ran one of his fraudulent operations from prison, that's how blatant he is.

"Do I look like I give a fuck". replied Dave.

At this point the employees brother who also worked at Anglia came out in support.

"You can fuck off". said Dave.

The brother looked at his sibling and then at Dave and decided to return to the showroom.

"That's right, jog on". said the scouse bloke as he walked away.

That was the crux of the conversation and it must have made an impression because a day later I got a phone call. I was clearing fish tanks from the basement of an aquarium on Commercial Road in the east end when the phone rang. It was Mr Whitchurch.

"Some of your friends came to the showroom yesterday". He said.

"Oh you've met my brother". I replied.

"I don't appreciate people coming on to my premises and threatening my employees". he said.

"I don't appreciate doing a job and not getting paid". I responded.

"Well you still haven't sent me an invoice for the work done.". Now he was starting to annoy me. He was playing games. We both knew the score, he thought that he could get away without paying me and now even after having the situation laid out to him in black and white he was still trying to worm his way out of it. The man is a bully and he was used to getting his own way, well not this time.

"Look Mick" I said "you either pay me or don't pay me but if you don't pay me my friends are coming back".

"Are you threatening me?" he said.

"No Mick" I replied "I am simply stating a fact".

"You still have some of my stuff". He had asked me to go back after to job was finished. There was a roll of old carpet and a wardrobe that I had got stuck in a lift on the last day of the job and the hotel had wanted it removed. It was junk, junk that I had been storing for him for the last three months. Oh and he hadn't paid me for that job either. I had had enough.

"Look Mick" I said "I am a busy man, do what you like, I have to go." and I hung up.

I stood there by the side of the busy London street trying to get a grip on what had just happened. I decided to phone Dave and tell him what had happened. His response was this, "Listen" he said "his little arsehole is going in and out". At that point my phone started beeping, I had another call coming in, I checked the caller ID. It was Whitchurch.

"Hello Mick." I said.

Only it wasn't Mick. It was his secretary. She wanted to know what my bank details were so that she could put the money in my account. Five minutes later and I had been paid in full. I did have to give Dave some money to pay the boys but he would accept nothing for himself. Me and Dave became really good friends after that, he even worked for me for a while and I will forever be in his debt. Not because he got my money back although god knows I needed it but because when I was at my lowest ebb he showed me that the bad guys don't always win. That if you are good and try to do the right thing there are people who will stand up for you. That there is such a thing as Karma even if it is a long game. I email Dave every week and visit him once a month. When he gets out of Wandsworth he wants to run the flower stall.

Ch. 12 This could be the last time

I spoke to Dave about the predicament I had regarding Mum in Spain. He wasn't in prison at the time and he said that he would be happy to go over with me or with another associate to pay Derick a visit in order to find out what the hell he was playing at. The problem I had was that I had decided to act in my Mum's best interests and I could not be sure that a bunch of heavies turning up and threatening her boyfriend would be that best way forward. My regular phone calls to Derick were becoming more and more difficult and now he was telling me that it was causing such grief with the sisters that it was probably better if I didn't call at all. At least for a little while. I did get to speak to Mum directly at these times but her conversation was becoming increasingly monosyllabic and it was difficult to understand exactly what she meant.

Aside from what was happening to Mum there was another factor to consider and that was the effect that all of this was having on my family. All of the time that this had been going on both Lisa and Molly had been nothing but supportive but nevertheless the situation was starting to take its toll. My concern for my Mum was having a negative effect on me although I'm not sure how well I could see it myself. It's kind of like the onset of madness. You don't notice because it happens so gradually. It's not like one day you are behaving in a perfectly rational manner and the next you are running down the street naked with your underpants on your head. It is a slow descent. Your behaviour today is remarkably similar to that of yesterday but it's a lot different to six months ago. It's like aging. Ten years ago my face was different to the one that I have now, yet it feels as if nothing has changed. It happens bit by bit. I have now come to the conclusion that even if I think I am normal, I'm probably not.

Lisa also found it frustrating that I didn't get angrier about things. I would tell her about what was going on in Spain and then she would become angrier than me. Then she would look at me incredulously because she couldn't understand why I wasn't hopping up and down. You know the kind of conversation. You tell your wife that your best friend is getting on your nerves, she backs you up by saying what a pain they are, you say "hang on they are not that bad" and then you have a row about it. You end up fighting the person who was trying to support you.

Regarding Mum's situation I felt powerless which is a very frustrating feeling. I had elected to put Mum's best interests first and the effect on my family was becoming intolerable. There was only one thing left to do. I would sever all communication with Spain after all it was what they wanted. Any inheritance I was due could go. I wouldn't call Mum to see how she was and try to make her laugh to brighten up her day and when the time came I wouldn't even go to the funeral. They could carry on with their own lives without me and I would stay here and look after my family. This was not an easy decision to make. I would ring Mum one last time and ask her if this is what she wanted. If it was then that is what I would do.

I rung on a Thursday morning. It was around ten o'clock, which was eleven Spanish time. I had been meaning to ring for all of the previous hour but the butterfly's in my stomach had stopped me. I knew that if I left it much later they may go out so it had to be now. Mum and Derick were now back in their own home, apparently living with Linda had not gone as smoothly as they had hoped. I had asked Derick what had gone wrong but as usual he had been vague. He said that things just didn't work out with all of them there and that Linda's cooking had been terrible. Sounds like an excuse to me. So much for 'if it was my father then I would take care of him'. Still at least she got a free en-suite out of it eh.

The international ring tone buzzed and Derick answered.

"Hello". he said in his singy Scottish accent.

"Can I speak to Mum please Derick". I said, my pulse racing. He passed me over. I asked her if she was okay and she said yes. Actually she said "yeeees". She had developed a very long drawn out yes, you know the kind that you do when you are trying to explain something to a child and rather than the usual clipped version. I think she made it longer because it was one of the few words that she could recall easily and she wanted to hold on to it for as long as possible.

"Mum I have to I have to talk to you about something". I said.

"Yeeees".

"Mum Derick says that my calling you is causing you stress and I am in a terrible position because I want to talk to you but I don't want to do anything that might upset you".

"Yeees".

"He doesn't even think that I should ring you anymore mum".

"Yeees".

"Is that what you want mum".

"Yeees".

My world fell to pieces. It was as though a steel spike had been pushed through my entire body. I felt a mixture of helplessness, inevitability and extreme sadness. I started to cry, but I swallowed it down. In truth I didn't really believe what I had just heard. I had asked my Mum if she never wanted me to call her again but I didn't really believe that she would ever say yes. Our relationship might have been tricky but there are many much worse than ours. To be told by your own mother that she doesn't want you any more is one of life's low points. What could I do. I said I would put Mum first and if this is what she wanted this is what I would have to do. Somewhat incredulous I choked back the tears and uttered in broken words.

"Okay mum, if that is what you want I understand. I love you mum".

There was no reply the phone just went quiet. Mum had passed it back to Derick. It was at that point that Derick said in his upbeat Scottish accent "So Peter, when are you and Jude coming over?"

I like many others I used to like 'Game for a Laugh' in the eighties. Don't judge me wind ups were popular then. Okay you put individuals through extreme pain and worry but it is worth it to see the look on their face at the end when they realise that the van holding all of their worldly goods that just got pushed into a river was not actually their van at all. Furthermore, the bloke on the corner in the policeman's outfit with a fake beard and a funny hand is actually in on the joke. He is about to reveal himself and explain that the van that you just saw was in fact a replica, brought in for the benefit of the wheeze, all much to the relief and delight of the van driver. My life was turning into the live version of Game for a Laugh and let me tell you the relief does not negate the stress and it isn't funny.

Thirty seconds ago I was saying goodbye to my mother forever and now I was being asked when am I getting on a plane. Or at least that is how it stood at the moment. Knowing Derick by the time I got home from market we might no longer be welcome and they might be moving to Cancun. Still at least for the moment things were looking up. I would get to see Mum. I could make sure that she was alright. I could start to remove the crazy images in my mind and replace them with reality, hopefully normality. I was also very much aware that time was precious and any time I could get with Mum must be treasured. I must also confess that part of me was a little disappointed. Thirty seconds ago all this was over. I could draw a line under it and move on, it would no longer affect me and mine. Despite my best efforts and through no fault of my own I had been released of all responsibility, a responsibility that was clearly mine. Now that responsibility had returned and if I am totally honest there was a part of me that was actually disappointed. I am not only a shit son I really am a shit human being.

I brought a cabin bag. I had watched George Clooney in 'Up in the Air' and I had been rather impressed. It is a film about baggage and the cabin bag is a simile. In the film George's character theorises that most of us carry around suitcase amounts of attachments in the form of family and friends and responsibilities and mortgages and debts.

He asks the question "How much does your life weigh? Then he goes on to expand on the metaphor. First he just considers material possessions, starting with things like your bedroom lamp and then ultimately moves up to your car and your house. Then he says put them all in an imaginary bag and then try to lift it. You can't. Then he says 'I'm now going to set the bag on fire' and asks what we would remove. We all immediately think photos but he says that that's for people who can't remember. George's character posits that there is nothing worth saving. Let the whole lot burn and then imagine waking up in the morning with nothing. It's actually quite an exciting thought.

He then goes one step further and tells us to fill the bag with people. Starting with casual acquaintances and then moving on to our nearest and dearest. Fortunately, he doesn't ask us to set them on fire but he does point out how much people also weigh us down with the daily compromises. The secrets we keep and the lies we tell. Ultimately Georges character concludes that we are better off alone and uses the animal analogy that we are not swans but sharks.

If you haven't seen the film, you should, it's very good. In the film Georges character's life was light. Milan Kundera wrote a book about this, it was called 'The Unbearable Lightness of Being'. In the book he states that life is divided into dualities like: 'good and bad' or 'day and night'. In most cases it is easy to work out which is the desirable one and which is not but he posits that this is not true for light and heavy. The book then goes on to tell the story of a doctor whose life and relationships are all very light until by accident he becomes properly involved with a lady. Milan concludes that a light life is ultimately unbearable, hence the title and that real relationships and a life that carries weight is what should be sort after and I agree. I know that Georges characters prescription is not the way to live life but right now I have to say the 'Up in the Air' approach was looking very tempting.

The real reason that I bought a cabin bag was because it makes perfect sense. It means that you can avoid the carousel bit. I have never understood people on planes. The second the wheels hit the tarmac and long before the fasten your safety belt lights have been switched off they are up in the aisles, popping open the overhead lockers and grabbing their bags ready to stampede off the plane. These are the same people who you then catch up with ten minutes later, clustered in groups and swaying like fatigued zombies as they wait for their big suitcases to emerge from the magic portal at the end of the carousel. You might get off the plane quickly, your luggage wont.

Besides we were going for three days and two nights. In Spain. In the sunshine. How many clothes would I need? Linen trousers short sleeve shirts and flip flops. We could have gone for longer but Jude had Lilly, I had work and more than that we had no idea how this trip was going to go. What if we got there and within the first ten minutes a massive row broke out and we didn't see each other for the rest of the trip. It was kind of a cross between a fact finding mission and a peace envoy. All of the factors you want present when you are off to visit your dying mother.

Funny thing travel. For my entire life the only time I ever found myself at an airport was when I was going on holiday. I know that people travel for work and conferences and such but I believe that most people are just like me and I behaved accordingly. Within half an hour of reaching the airport me and Jude were at the bar, her with a large gin and tonic and me with a pint of Stella. It was seven o'clock in the morning but the second you get through security you are no longer on British soil. You are in fact in a twilight zone where taxes on booze and fags shouldn't apply and commonly held attitudes to drinking premium lager soon after dawn go right out of the window. Its maritime law, at least that's the way I look at it. But as the day drew on I felt less and less like drinking. This was partly down to the trepidation over what would be waiting for us on the other side and from a slightly more noble point of view I was going to see my Mum, I hadn't seen her for months. I was looking forward to it and I wasn't about to turn up pissed.

I think it's the first time ever that I have been anxious about landing. I like flying. When I was a kid I always wanted to be an astronaut. More specifically I wanted to be either a Star Ship Captain or a Robot Psychologist. I told this to the careers advisor at school. He told me that those jobs didn't actually exist and I said I know and that it wasn't my fault that we had all been lied to in the seventies. He then suggested that I try to become a normal ship's captain or a computer programmer but I was very specific. Star ship Captain or Computer Psychologist, I didn't want to be anything else. It was at that point that Mr Berol said "Get out Coath, there is nothing that I can do for you". I have to confess that I was surprised by his response and also remember feeling a little short changed. Looking back, I must have been a nightmare to deal with. Sorry Mr Berol.

I'm forty-six now so there is little to no chance of me ever going up in a rocket (although I haven't given up hope) but that bit where a plane goes from nought to one hundred and eighty must be a little bit like what it is like. When we take off I sometimes rock backwards and forwards in my seat trying to make the plane go faster. I say I like flying but to be honest the bit in-between take-off and landing is a bit dull. Fortunately, now I've got a kindle so I can prop it on the tray table in front of me and watch movies that I have illegally downloaded from the internet. Landing is fun too, particularly if they sway the plane from side to side as they sometimes do. This time was different though and the closer I came to the end of the flight the more nervous I became. Each little step of our journey brought me closer to whatever lay behind the velvet curtain.

I was also on unfamiliar territory. We were flying into Gibraltar. I had flown to Spain many times in my life but it had always been into Malaga, the airport closest to our flat and then later on to Mum's. Problem was that because we were flying out of season, there were no flights between Luton and Malaga at times that worked for me and Jude, so it had to be Gib. We departed the plane with our pull a longs and entered the small, shack like airport. There was a brief pause at the duty free while I debated whether to buy the small allotted amount of Marlboro lights for Lisa or to take a chance and buy loads but then risk getting caught and fined. I went for the former and it came as no surprise when I then walked through the rest of the airport without seeing one single official from customs and excise. Once leaving the airport it is only a short walk into Spanish territory. Once there we would have to face the task of how best to do the hour journey to the Costa del sol. It was then that my phone rang. It was Derick. He had come to meet us.

The call left me with mixed emotions. The journey to Marbella, where Mum lived would have been long and costly and the fact that Derick had made the effort to come and see us would make life a lot easier. On the other side of things, it meant that if anything was going to kick off it would kick off now, a lot sooner than I had expected or been prepared for. Once I walked through the small metal gate that took me from English territory to Spanish my unease grew. It was like I was previously on my turf and now I was on his. This feeling is ridiculous especially because Derick is from Scotland. He's lived in Spain for nearly twenty years and his accent is as broad now as it was the day he left. We walked a short way towards the busy dual carriageway that fed from Spain into Gibraltar. Crossing it was a smaller road which formed a crossroads and on the corner was an airstream style American diner. I imagined being in California or New York, anywhere but here. It wasn't just the uncertainty of how it might go, I was about to see my Mum again and I had no idea of how bad she would be, how far her illness had taken her since the last time that we met. It was then that my eyes focused on a more familiar sight. Outside the diner stood Derick.

He was wearing his usual outfit. Fine V necked sweater, open collar shirt, Farah's and a pair of hush puppy style comfortable shoes. All in matching muted shades of grey. A polar opposite to the bloke in the novel by the same name. He stood on the spot shifting from foot to foot, either out of nerves or just as a way of passing the time. He saw us and called out his usual highland 'Hello' and we closed the space between us to meet him. Derick said that the car was a little way from the airport through a park in a car park and that Mum was in the car. It was at this point that the dark side reared its ugly head again. As we started to walk away from the main throng and into what can only be described as scrubland (they don't get a lot of rain out there) I started to think: Where is he taking us? Is Mum really there or is this a setup? Instead of Mum are we about to meet Linda and Jane who are here to tell me what a shit human being I am or worse maybe it will be a gang of heavies who have come to give me a good hiding, is it an ambush? Surely not. Even as I write this I realise how ridiculous it sounds. We live in the real world and these things don't happen in the real world. Even in my real world it only happened once but at the time my head was in such a weird place that anything, no matter how strange was not inconceivable. What actually happened was we did a very short walk over some dusty brown ground to a tarmac car park. In that car park was a Renault Scenic and there in the front seat was Mum.

She was sitting in the front perched on the seat like old fashioned lady with her handbag on her lap. When she saw us she moved to get out of the car which was a struggle. Her mobility had not improved and she had put on weight as a consequence. Still she looked well. Her hair was pretty much intact and her face was still relatively thin. Most importantly Mum was fine. It's the strange thing with people, their appearance can change dramatically and yet they still to look like themselves and there is something very consoling in that. I hugged her and we did the awkward quick hello thing and then took our places in the car for the hour's drive back to Fuengirola and the bar, familiar territory.

The 'carreteria' that runs along the south coast of Spain is a very fast road. In fact, I believe that it has had more fatalities than any other road in the whole of Europe but it felt perfectly safe today. As we came nearer to the Costa de Sol the road draws closer to the coast until it runs parallel with the sea. I sat in the back of the Renault with the windows open looking out to where a blue ocean met a bright blue sky and of the first time in months I felt a kind of tranquillity. For the first time in a long time things were looking just a little bit rosier.

We got to the bar where Derick had a few things to sort out and this gave me and Jude enough time to go round the corner and check into the pension style hotel that we had booked into. The place was sparse and basic but also clean and perfectly functional. We regrouped at the bar and set off to Mum's house for lunch. My Mum has always prided herself on her cooking and rightly so. Particularly desserts. She made the best lemon meringue pie, her crème caramel was a delight, her raspberry Pavlova was something to behold and it's not many people who can pull of a baked Alaska. Unfortunately her cooking days had rather fallen by the way side, what with the illness but we still had a fabulous buffet to look forward to. When we got to the house the four of us sat in the outside on the white garden furniture, slowly making our way through prawns and smoked salmon and various other delights while making pleasant conversation and with absolutely no mention of 'I don't think that you should call', what the fuck was that all about?' That is the way that it is. The things that you think you will say you don't and certainly for now I was content with that. Near the end of the meal Mum was flagging. The long journey to Gibraltar had taken it out of her and so Derick took us back to Fuengirola. Despite her tiredness Mum still came along for the trip, I guess any time spent together is good time.

It was on the journey home that Derick dropped the bombshell. He said that he wanted to meet us at the bar about half past ten the next morning because he had an appointment at the solicitors, he wanted to give me power of attorney over Mum's estate. This was fabulous news. It put aside any fears that I might of had about Derick having an ulterior motive and it also meant that Mums future would now definitely be safe. I would be in charge of the money. I trust me, I can I'm trustworthy. When we got back to the bar I kissed my Mum good bye and told her that I would see her tomorrow. As the car drove away me and Jude waved the two of them goodbye, then we went and got pissed. It had been a hell of a day.

There is a Roger McGough poem. It goes something like this:

When I am away from you I feel a deep emptiness, a desperate longing.

When I am with you I get the reassuring feeling of wanting to escape.

Seeing Mum had been great but it had been difficult. Conversation was pleasant but there was still an underlying fear of not really knowing what was going on. Perhaps the visit to the solicitors in the morning would solve that. For the rest of the afternoon me and Jude got slowly drunk. Well after all we had a lot to discuss. There is a beautiful big square in the centre of Fuengirola where both the Spanish and tourists sit and drink while admiring the ancient church in the centre and where the shocking pink bougainvillea drapes itself over the bus stops that surround the square. There is also a much smaller square around the corner where mainly the Spanish go. It is behind the old post office, in itself an imposing building, and while not being as grand as the larger square it is perfectly formed. We sat there. We talked about what we thought of the situation and general life. How Jude was doing down in Cornwall and how Lilly and Molly were. All the time Jude sank Spanish measures of gin and tonic and I moved from San Miguel to whisky. The alcohol came as a welcome relaxant to the pent up emotion that I had been feeling, or maybe that was just an excuse. I even started smoking again, albeit only for the duration of the trip. I am shit at smoking. It makes me feel sick and when I smoke I look like a girl but never the less there I was working my way through Jude's Benningtons. Make of it what you will, all I know is that it all came as quite a relief.

We got up with plenty of time to spare so as not to be late for the appointment at the solicitors. As usual my mood was a combination of hope, dread and what the fuck. We struggled to find a coffee place near the bar that was open before ten and then ended up rushing our coffee's to make sure that we were on time. Derick and Mum arrived forty minutes late and it turned out that we were not going to the solicitors now, plans had changed. This is what it was always like with Derick. Not exactly moving the goal posts more like goal posts that were constructed on boats that were set adrift in a turbulent ocean. They didn't just move; half of the time you didn't even know if they were there.

Instead of going to the solicitors we kicked around the bar and then went for lunch in the main square. Over the lunch the tranquillity returned. You reach a stage, after constant battery, where you think 'do you know what I am tired of this, what will be will be'. After all we were sitting in a beautiful square in Spain, the sun was shining and I was with my Mum. You know that people say make the most of life because you never know when things might change. Well I knew that things were going to change very soon and I intended to make the most of this time. Despite her protests I

112

bought her the biggest bouquet of lilies and white roses that I could from the flower booth on the corner. It was the least I could do as Mum would insist on paying for everything. The buffet, the lunch in the square and the evening meal were all on Mum, I felt the need to do something. After lunch we had to go to a medical centre where Mum was due to get some physio. It was then that I started to see how life really was for Mum and Derick.

Derick drove us to a health centre on the outskirts of Fuengirola. It was a sleek new building made of glass and chrome. I am proud of our NHS and personally think that it is a wonderful thing but I have to say that the Spanish do it very well too. I helped Derick get Mum into the reception where some orderlies took her away for an hour of physio leaving Derick to try to sort out a mountain of paperwork, in pidgin English/Spanish with the lady on reception. Fifteen minutes later and with some success he sat down. I asked him if this is what is was like all of the time and he put his head in his hand and said "It's a nightmare Peter". Sorting out extreme cancer treatment for someone in your own country is difficult enough but sorting it out in a foreign country where your grip of the language is limited is a task and a half. What is the Spanish for sub temporal hematoma? It would help if you had someone who you could talk to who was properly fluent in Spanish but for Derick that was Linda so that was off of the table. At all times you needed to know where you need to be at what time and for what while taking which drugs. It's a full time job and clearly one that Derick had taken on fully and pretty much on his own. He said "Where are her friends Peter? Where are all of the people from the golf club? All of those who said that they would be there for Vicky and come round and visit all of the time. They're nowhere to be seen. I wouldn't mind if they would even ring from time to time but it is like she has dropped off of the planet". Then he said "Oh well never mind, we'll just have to get on with it". He wasn't really moaning for himself rather he was frustrated and angry on Mum's behalf for all of the people who claimed to be her friend who now had very little to do with her. Taking care of Mum was no easy feat and it was becoming clear that his devotion to my mother and all her needs was unwavering.

We went out for dinner that evening, Mum still liked the finer things in life but she was clearly struggling to keep up with it all. Nevertheless we went to Mum's favourite restaurant in fish alley, a place called Aroma where they serve food on triangle shaped plates and put a pansy in your salad so it must be posh. The meal was lovely and the company was fine even if we did cut it somewhat short. In the morning Mum and Derick took us to the airport and we said a fond farewell. Derick said that I should return soon as it was important for me to see as much of my mother as possible and it was good for Mum to see me. I said I would return in a month and we hugged.

When I got home I went around to my Dad's. I wanted to fill him in and to tell him that all was well in Spain, that Mum was being well looked after and that I intended to return in about a months' time. He was also pleased and relieved and he told me that he had a thousand Euros sitting in the safe that I could take with me the next time I went. After all he wasn't going to use them. He would have loved to have

114

gone out to visit Mum but he couldn't fly on account of the fact that he was also dying of a brain tumour. Oh didn't I mention that.

Part 2

Dad

Ch.1 A different kettle of fish altogether

My Dad was not like my Mum. He was generous, self-deprecating, optimistic, kind and funny. He worked very hard, enjoyed holidays and he loved a party. He was also very money orientated and fucked people who were not my Mum but all in all I liked my Dad. That is not to say that I didn't like my Mum, after all when you live with someone for over twenty years you can't help but have something in common. The thing is it's like Jude once said to her "you're a very difficult person to like Vicky". I think I am more like my Dad. We all display the traits of our parents whether we choose to admit it or not. I think the difference lies in the fact that if me and Mum spent too much time together it would probably end up in a row but from the age of fourteen I worked with my Dad every Saturday and we very rarely argued. We just got on with it.

Dad said to me once that he first realised something was wrong while he was on the phone to me. He said that we were in a middle of a phone conversation when I started to go quiet. His first reaction was 'what is wrong with this phone?' but then he looked down and realised that the reason that he could not hear me is because his arm had dropped away from his ear. He quickly pulled it up again but the fact remained that his body had started operating independently of his brain and that's not good. I get worried when my van starts making funny noises, I can't even begin to imagine what it must be like if it's your body that starts playing up.

119

The other thing that alerted my Dad to the fact that all was not well was also partly down to me. My Dad was a drummer and a proper musician. I play guitar a bit but it is purely for my own amusement and certainly not for the amusement of others but Dad was good. In the past he had played in a covers band called 'Stray Lightening'. I'm sure you have an image in your head right now and you are spot on. Social clubs, weddings and pubs playing sixties and seventies rock. Everybody put your hands in the air for 'high ho silver lining' and then we'll break for the bingo. He used to get up at five o'clock on a Saturday morning and go to market all day and then when he got home he would unload the van, fill it with the drums and go play a gig till midnight. When he got back to the house he would unload the drums, reload the van and then get up at five o'clock the next day to go to market again. I once asked him how he did it and he simply said that he enjoyed it, it didn't feel like work.

The band had been disbanded for some time now and Dad had his drums stored in boxes in the warehouse until one day I suggested that he set them up in the office. He loved playing them and he had nowhere to put them in his new house, the one he now lived in with my step-mum and besides drums are noisy, neighbours don't like drums. If he set the kit up he could practice while waiting for deliveries, he could get away from my step-mum when she was driving him mad because she was drunk again and there was the outside chance that we would get to play together. It was when he was practicing on the kit that he realised that he could no longer do certain rhythms that he used to do. His paradiddle was no longer paradiddleing. At the time he had put it down to being out of practice but with such things there is a little voice at the back your head that says 'it's not that and you know it's not.' His falling phone arm confirmed this.

I can't imagine how scary it must be when you suspect that there is something majorly wrong with you. I once saw a film starring Robert Carlyle called 'Go Now'. He played a young football player who was climbing a ladder with a hammer one day and the hammer just fell from his hand. What made the scene powerful was the expression on his face. It said 'I didn't mean to do that'. It turns out that his character has multiple sclerosis and the rest of the film takes you through the slow degeneration of his character. There was another scene much later in the film that has stayed with me. His condition had worsened and he and his fiancée had gone to a centre where he was due to receive treatment. In the centre were people whose condition was much worse than his, one individual who couldn't control his body. Our hero looked horrified and the other guy said "I know what you are thinking, if it was me I would just command my body not to do that, well it will happen to you and you can't". Something similar was going to happen to my Dad.

What must have made it even more troubling for my father is that he was already no stranger to cancer. Years ago the doctors had discovered cancer in one of his kidneys. If you have to get cancer in a major organ that's the one to go for. There's a good chance that the cancer didn't migrate anywhere else and you've got another one so they just give you some chemo and take it out, job done. Actually not job done as the cancer had migrated to his lungs. Fortunately you've got two of them as well and though you actually kind of need both you can lose bits of them, so they did an operation to remove the offending bits and hopefully that was that. No such luck, now the nasty little disease had moved up into his brain and you've only got one of those. However unlike Mum's brain tumour, Dad's tumour was small and on the outside of his brain so there was every chance that with chemotherapy and some minor operations that could remove it all once again and everything would be fine. At least that's what they tell you.

However cancer was the least of my Dad's problems, he had to live with my step-mum. Now let's face it at this point I am going to be a little bit bias as against the woman who broke up my parent's marriage but to be honest with you I'd like to think that I gave her every chance. The whole thing all started a long time ago.

When Mum and Dad were still together Mum would often do a Sunday roast. This would of course happen in the evening because Dad would be at work during the day. Me and Lisa would sometimes join them and to be honest these times would have been more often if it wasn't for Mum's tendency to have too much to drink and then say something stupid. Mum and Dad would then have a row and Mum would put herself to bed. On one such occasion I said to him "I don't know how you put up with it". It's very difficult to come back from a statement like that.

I first got the earth shattering news when I was driving home from work one Saturday afternoon. I was a couple of junctions away from home when the phone rang and I answered it. You were never allowed to talk on the mobile while driving but back then it wasn't considered to be such a big deal, a bit like drinking and driving in the seventies. It was Mum. She was ringing to tell me that she had found out that Dad was having an affair and that they were splitting up. Of course being my family that's not how the conversation went. No what she actually said was "Peter, is there any chance that you can go to work with your dad tomorrow instead of me as me I won't work with your dad, I've just found out that he is having an affair". Still reeling from the news I asked Mum to put Dad on. At this point you still think that it's not actually happening, that it is some kind of practical joke that is about to be revealed much to my personal relief, good old Beadle. Dad came on the phone and said in an excited voice. "Yeah it's true mate, your old mans in love". I remember thinking two things at the time. Firstly: 'you don't have to sound so happy about it'. I'm sure he was, in fact I'm sure he was ecstatic but that doesn't mean that he had to show it so explicitly, particularly while you are standing next to my Mum. Secondly, was his use of the term 'your old man'. My Dad never referred to himself this way before. All I can think of is that there are certain times in our lives where we feel somewhat out of control and these are the times that we say or do things that two seconds later we say to ourselves 'what did you say that for?' When you are thirteen and you go to speak to that girl that you like for the first time or if you meet someone famous. God knows I've done it enough times. I turned down the offer of work with Dad the next day. Partly because after the news of the moribund marriage I could hardly jump straight to my father's support, what kind of a message would that have sent to my mother. Also I didn't relish the idea of spending the day with my Dad while he would be extra nice to me because he felt guilty and we would inevitably go through what had happened. In all honesty the main reason that I turned it down was because we had friends coming round for dinner and I was rather looking forward to it. Turns out that even when my world turns upside down I am still selfish.

Maybe I am being a little bit harsh on myself, truth of the matter is that like Mum and Dad I was also reeling from this new revelation. I was not surprised to find out that my Dad was not whiter than white. What surprised me was that it would in any way affect their marriage. They had been together for twenty-seven years. When a couple have been together that long they pretty much stay together even if they can't stand each other. I have heard stories of widows at wakes that are actually relieved that they no longer have to put up with his snoring and the way he squashes the peas onto his knife, widows who are looking forward to finally living their life. Well if that's the case don't wait until he dies, dump him now. Why live in a world of abject misery if you don't have to? And don't stay together for the sake of the kids, that's just daft. That's like saying I want my misery to affect everyone. It's almost as if misery loves company. Oh. Anyway I think that miserable people stay together because they are lazy and scared. They have become accustomed to the person they are with and they are frightened of being on their own. That and they haven't found another woman's underwear in the Ali baba basket. It kind of forces your hand.

Truth is that in my heart of hearts I didn't really believe their marriage to be over. I assumed that Dad might move out for a bit and then come back to Mum, maybe not on his hands and knees but at least marginally apologetic and Mum, who clearly still loved him would take him back. What I didn't expect to happen was for Dad to carry on living in the matrimonial home for another week getting everything into place before leaving. I went round to see them on the Monday to find out what was going on, to find Dad on the

125

driveway building a false floor in the new van. Mum even brought him out a cup of coffee. Surely what you are supposed to do is throw all of their worldly belongings out on to the lawn, set fire to them and then piss on them. Do something outrageous. Cut an arm or leg from all of the clothes in his wardrobe, It's the only chance you will ever have to do it without getting locked up. What you are not supposed to do is carry on with business as usual. I went round on the Thursday night and Mum had cooked dinner and they were both eating it on trays in front of the telly. I think that she believed that if everything carried on as normal that he just wouldn't leave. She was wrong. He did. The following weekend he moved out of Mums and in with the woman who sold the jewellery on Stevenage market.

I knew her as I had worked Stevenage for Dad. Her name was Beverley or as Mum came to christen her 'the poisoned dwarf'. I believe this is a Dallas reference but I never watched Dallas as I spent Friday nights with my Grandma who watched Dynasty and the two clashed. Mum would drop me off on Friday after school and then in the evening Grandad would go down the Stopsley Working Men's club and I would watch Dynasty with Grandma and then the snooker. I would spend Friday nights with my Grandma so that Mum and Dad could spend a night alone together. They were happy then.

Beverley or Miss Beverley or the poisoned dwarf, the pseudonyms are many, was thirteen years younger than my Dad and therefore only seven years older than me. Of course I applied all of the usual jokes about midlife crisis and

126

swapping for a younger model. For the first three years I went out of my way to find a birthday card with red sports cars on the cover, not that it was appreciated. Nevertheless I had said that I didn't know how Dad and Mum were still together and although I didn't appreciate how the break up came about, once an appropriate time had passed, I thought it would be the right thing to do to go out for a meal with Dad and his new girlfriend.

The thing about crazy people is that it is often not obvious, it's subtle. It's not crazy all of the time it's crazy some of the time. It's certain things that they do or sometimes something that they say that makes you think 'that was a bit strange'. It's times like these that you start to realise that there is a crazy curtain behind which lies their real self. Everyone else may see them as normal they are not. I also think that part of the problem is that most people have terrible social skills. They don't look and they don't listen. They deserve to have their tufty club membership revoked. How many times have you had a conversation with someone who suddenly starts talking about something totally unrelated? The reason for this is because they were not actually listening to you but instead they were spending all of the time that you were talking working out what they were going to say next. A skill for which my Mum was the world's leading authority.

I have a customer who I affectionately refer to as Susan the Lesbian because her name is Susan and she is a lesbian. She is terribly guilty of this. She used to turn up every Thursday and tell me about everything that is wrong in the world. She was loud and oblivious to the effect that her forthright opinions were having on the surrounding customers. It wasn't just that she didn't care, she couldn't see it despite the fact that she actually believed that she was a highly perceptive individual. I remember one particular rhetoric where she was preaching about how women's social skills were so much better than men's and for the entire rant all that was going through my head was 'shut up, shut up, shut up, shut up'. She was totally oblivious. I believe that on the whole women's social skills are better than men's. Just not hers.

Of course some people are really good at concealing the madness. Otherwise there would be no serial killers. We would all just point and shout, "quick, arrest that nutter". I have a friend who I call earworm Nige because he is the world's best at putting a tune in your head. On the market it's a bit like that, we all get nick names. Colin the fruit, Michael the towels, Paul the cheese (who sells pizzas). Sometimes your commodity is superseded by your race like Indian Mick or Jewish Andy. I once decided that this wasn't right and decided to reprogram my mobile changing his name from Jewish Andy to Andy the Jewellery but because it was one of those old Nokia phones that only took twelve characters it still came out as Andy the Jew.

Earworm Nige is a manic depressive. So is his sister but unlike his sister he doesn't take the correctional pills. You see Nige is a bit of a musician. He doesn't get to play as much as he would like but he believes that if he took the pills it would take his inspiration away. Despite not being on the pills he has learned to project an image. He works with me and to all of the customers he comes across as one of the happiest people that you could ever wish to meet. I know him better. Some days after being jolly at work all day he goes home, crawls into bed, turns the lights off and pulls the covers over his head. If he hadn't told me this, I would never have known. Beverley, my step-mum, not so skilled.

On the first time that we went out together as two couples she was weird from the start. You kind of make excuses for it like maybe she is nervous or just not got a grip on the mood yet. We had not long sat down to have our meal when she turned to Lisa and said "I know what would be fun, let's talk like Americans, then the waitress will think that we are American". Okay firstly what? and secondly the waitress won't think we are Americans on the grounds that she has been serving us for the last twenty minutes where we have been speaking in our normal accents. All the waitress will think is that you're a looney. For the rest of the evening the conversation progressed peppered by me and Lisa casting sideways looks at each other thinking what did she say that for? It's not just strange responses. One of my drinking buddies from my late teens was a guy called Tim. He had a tendency to say and do strange things at the wrong time, of course he did, he went to private school. Thing is it didn't matter because his heart was always in the right place and you knew that he always meant well. What was more worrying about Beverley's comments was that they weren't just out of place, they were somehow, wrong. Even saying that strange behaviour on its own is not exactly harmful and perhaps given time we could have worked a way round it. We may have come to accept it as one of her eccentricities and made a fist

of it for the sake of my Dad. That was of course if it hadn't
been for her drinking.

Ch3. Viva Espagna

Living with cancer is hard enough. Living with cancer and a drunken wife means that you are fighting a war on two fronts. Which came first the cancer or the drinking? The drinking.

Dad and Beverley stayed together for years. They were married for twelve years and they were together for four years before that. Dad had said that he would never marry again and Beverley said that she never wanted to be married. They all say that. 'I don't want to be married and I don't want children, I am happy just the way we are'. Then after a while the conversation turns to the hypothetical. 'If we were to get married, not that we are, I wonder where we would have it and what it would be like?' Once that's out there you may as well get yourself straight down to Moss Bros because it's as good as done. In the end Dad did ask Beverley to marry him. He said that it was for Spanish tax reasons but I believe that there was more to it than that. I believe that in the beginning they were happy together, in the beginning he loved her. I also think that a lot of it came down to lust. I remember once visiting the house. Mum had moved out to the flat in Spain and Beverley had moved into the house with my Dad. Beverley is a cuckoo. It wasn't just my Dad that she fell for but the whole package. The big house, the range rover, the exotic holidays and I don't blame her for this. Love exists in a context not a vacuum. People say I would love you if you were short or tall, fat or thin, rich or poor but that's all bollocks. I remember once watching an episode of Ricky Lake where this guy had married and within a year his wife had nearly doubled in weight. He was on the show saying that he just didn't fancy her anymore. Being Ricky Lake the whole audience was crucifying the poor guy and telling him that he should love his wife for the woman that she is on the inside. His response was 'I know, but I don't fancy her anymore'. At least he was being honest. Besides the guy was right, people change and what is to say that you are going to like what they change into. Suppose the person that you are with reads Mien Kampf and decides to become a fully-fledged member of the Nazi party, are you still supposed to love them then? It may sound ridiculous but my in-laws were staunch Labour supporters for most of their adult life, in the last election they voted UKip.

Beverley saw what my Mum had, decided that she wanted that for herself and took it. For Dad I believe that it was a relationship fuelled by lust. He is after all a typically seventies man. Midlife crisis fucks his secretary, that kind of thing. To back up this statement I was once in the hallway of their house outside the bedroom. I looked up and screwed into the lintel and preventing the door from shutting was a large hook. I said "what's the hook for?" And then a split second later I added "don't answer that". They just laughed but now there is an enduring image in my head that I wish that I could erase.

I also think that along with the wild sex came the booze. The two kind of go hand in hand and as I have already mentioned Dad did love a party. I wonder how much of it was the monster cometh and how much of it was you created a monster. Dad's requirement always seemed to be: cook, cleaner, whore and market trader. Mum used to work two days a week, Beverley would go to work with Dad three days a week. Mum developed a drink problem and used to hide the brandy bottles in the airing cupboard, Beverley would hide the empty bottles of white wine all over the house. Now bearing in mind that he only had two wives and they both ended up the same way it is rather a question of did they jump or were they pushed. Actually no it isn't. No one was holding a gun to their head. They drank because they chose to. I have heard it said that drinking is an illness and I have to be honest this annoys the hell out of me. My best friend's mum has MS. For the last twenty-five years her body has slowly given up to that stage that now she is confined to a wheelchair with practically no use of her limbs but despite this she bears her affliction with good spirits. MS is an illness. If you told Anne that if she stopped pouring a certain liquid into her body all of her problems would go away then she would. Don't tell me alcoholism is an illness, it insults the ill. No alcoholics are not ill they are addicts and addictions can be broken. All you need to do is recognise that your dependency is ruining your life and the lives of those who care for you and then have the will power to stop, but you have got to want to stop. If you don't then just admit that you are too weak and don't blame anyone else. Everyone's got a story and were can all blame others for our own shortcomings. If you choose to come up short at least have the decency to be honest.

Truth is Beverley's drinking started long before Dad's cancer. It was present from the very beginning. When she was younger she had been a bit of a party girl so booze and coke were a standard. My parents were never drug people so when she paired up with Dad any banned substances went by the wayside. However as far as alcohol was concerned, fill your boots. This situation was also massively accelerated by their move to Spain.

Dad and Beverley were becoming fed up with the markets. Life is like that. Even if you are a rock star eventually you get fed up with all of the days on tour, all of the hanging around airports and staying in hotels until you decided to turn the whole thing in, buy a farm and make cheese. And market trading is not an easy life. The mornings are early and the days are long. We are often exposed to harrowing weather conditions, terrible traffic and worse than all of that are the punters. People who believe that £1 is too much to pay for a 100% cotton t-shirt whilst holding a cup of coffee that probably cost over double that. Of course some people are nice and appreciate you but most think that it is some kind of game where because they are on a market it is their duty to haggle. I tell you now guys we hate that. The stuffs cheap enough, if you want to barter go the Marrakesh. I know the exact time that Dad lost patience with the markets. He had just finished a five-minute argument with two ladies who wanted two pairs of jogging bottoms for a fiver because they were 'buying in bulk' and he turned round and saw what looked like a nice old lady stick a pack of socks in her bag and walk off the stall. As he recounted the story to me he said "Peter, I just don't want to do it anymore".

Dad and Beverley decided to move to Spain to be estate agents. On the face of it this might seem like a giant leap, from Wilsden to the Costa Del Sol but only if you haven't seen the film Sexy Beast. If you haven't seen it then you should. It's got Ray Winstone, Ian McShane and Ben Kinglsley playing a part that should have won him an Oscar. In the opening sequence Ray Winstone is lying by the pool of a rather expensive villa beneath a pure blue azure sky and shortly after his wife turns up in a convertible Mercedes carrying handfuls of designer shopping bags. Shortly after Ben Kinglsey turns up and the whole thing goes tits. Nevertheless for the beginning part of the film Ray and the missus are living la vita facile and I think it is this idea that Dad and Beverley fell in love with. People do that. They fall in love with ideas not realities and once you get an idea into your head you start to imagine the way things would be. Dad was going to take the Spanish property market by storm. Beverley would ride palomino horses and paint watercolour scenes. It's a bit like when you buy a home gym because if you had one of those then you would get fit. No you won't. If you are already doing press up and sit ups and running round the street and you want to get a home gym to help yourself get fit then you'll use it. If you think by buying a home gym you will fit, what you will actually get is a really expensive clothes horse.

As far as Dad was concerned he may have been a great market trader but when it came to property he was a genius at making exactly the wrong decision. He sold the big house that I lived in the latter part of my youth when the market was at rock bottom and then moved into rented for six years while house prices went through the roof. Then he bought a small bungalow in Whipsnade with a six-acre wood attached and no possibility of planning permission. Three years later he sold it for what it cost him to a tree hugger and moved to Spain. I don't think Donald Trump has much to worry about on that score. As for Beverley's belief that if she moved to Spain she would paint watercolours and ride horses, she lived in Whipsnade, it's the horse riding capital of south England. No what they thought would happen didn't happen. What actually happened was that they found themselves in a remote finca in the la Cala mountains with little to do and a constant stream of friends coming over on holiday all expecting a party. There's one thing that you will do in Spain and that's drink.

The thing about drink is it's addictive. Like the man said 'I'm not into drugs, I'm happy with me beer and me fags'. It's a drug, all the best things are. I know that we are supposed to drink water and eat fruit. I don't like fruit. I have a theory on fruit. The only reason that people eat fruit is because it is low in calories and it's good for you. If chocolate or chips were low in calories and good for you fruit would rot on the trees. There they were out in Spain with little to do and a constant supply of cheap alcohol. It was only going to go one way. Dad kept it under control. They did have an Estate office and during the days Dad would go to work but when he came home Beverley was drunk.

What he could never understand was why she drunk on her own. He said "I can understand it if we are out having a good time but where's the attraction of sitting on your own drinking?" I know the answer to this. The reason I know the answer to this is because I have that monster within me. Fortunately for me I have a wonderful wife. Every time I have looked close to going off of the rails the reins have been firmly pulled in and for that I am grateful. My problem is that if I start I don't want to stop. Have one biscuit, eat the packet so the answer is simple, don't start. Problem is, I like drinking, it stops my head from whirring. If I am not drinking I am constantly looking around for something that needs doing through a combination of restlessness and guilt. I eventually found that the best thing for me is that I now only drink at weekends. Strangest thing is that you imagine that when you get to Friday you would be chaffing at the bit to get a drink down you but what you actually end up thinking is 'I've done four days, seems a shame to break the streak now.' You see extreme drinkers know they shouldn't do it. But the devil inside you is clever and it says 'I'll just have the one and then I'll stop.' 'I'll just have one more and then I'll stop'. Then, as you have more to drink, your resolve starts to go until it all goes out of the window and before you know it you're pissed.

Then you have to try to hide it, act sober because if you don't then you won't be able to do it next time. The problem is when your drunk it's very difficult to act sober, because your drunk. Once your partner points out your state you then take various different defensive tacks. Denial 'I'm not pissed'. Aggression 'I work hard and I'm not hurting anybody, why do you always have to keep attacking me'. Compliance 'I know, I'm sorry I won't to do it again'. You'll say anything to get out of the situation. You even believe it yourself. I'll have a drink today but then I'll start calming it down tomorrow. Have you ever noticed how it's always tomorrow? I'll go on a diet tomorrow. I'll stop smoking tomorrow. I'll buy these shoes and that will be my lot. That's how the devil works.

Dad and Beverley were in Spain for about four years. They bought a load of development land in inland Spain just before the Spanish property crash. He lost a lot of money and she became an alcoholic. All of time they were there they lived in a beautiful Spanish farm house up in the hills of La Cala, overlooking a sweeping valley under the Spanish sun. A beautiful villa that could be easily located by the large mobile phone mast that overshadowed it. They say those things cause cancer, could be a coincidence, we'll never know.

Ch. 4 Milk Churn Gate

Dad and Beverley returned to England and bought a small place around the corner from us near the warehouse and went back to work on the markets. It was soon after that his cancer was diagnosed. Like I say the first two bouts he took in his stride. He went for the operations, took the pills and carried on working as best he could. But third time it was nasty. The cancer was on the outside of his brain and so they could treat it with something they called a cyber-knife. I never really got to the bottom of it but I always imagined it to be some Tron like machine that removed the cancer in a virtual world but in the real world it didn't. On top of the machine there was the chemo. Now as I understand it, chemotherapy is now a lot better than it used to be. It now comes in tablet form rather than in the old days where they used to just blast you with radiation, a bit like Bill Bixby in the incredible hulk.

Chemotherapy kills cancer. The problem is that it kills you too, it just kills you slower. When I was young and fell over and scraped my knees my Mum used to ask me if she should punch me in the arm, that way the pain in my arm would be so great that I would forget about the pain in my knee. You know in the films when they say to the hostage "if you give us the information we need we can make your death a quick and painless one, otherwise it will be a slow painful drawn out death". Seems to me that if you ask this question to a cancer patient they would opt for the latter. Of course I am being flippant. With the drugs you get two weeks on and two weeks off. For half the time you feel relatively well and for the other half you have to endure ulcers, discomfort and tiredness. It's better than the alternative. What should not be one of the side effects of taking cancer reducing drugs is a drunken wife.

I used to pick my Dad up on a Monday morning from round the corner from his home and take him to the warehouse. I would ask him how things were and then he would tell me about Beverley's drinking. At first she only went off of the rails once a week, then it turned into twice a week and then most of the time. At least that is what he told me. I wonder exactly how much he let on. He was always an honest person and if you asked him for an answer he would give it to you straight but there are times when we don't always let on, whether it is because we are embarrassed of the situation that we have got ourselves into, or because we don't want to appear to be moaning all of the time, or simply because we don't want to burden the person that we are talking to with our problems. Also I think he still loved her and so probably wanted to protect her. At least for a while anyway. He would tell me that when she was sober she was great. She couldn't do enough for him, she would make sure that he was comfortable and that she used to create wonderful meals. In fact, the cooking is kind of how her problem seemed to start. He would say that she would go into the kitchen to cook dinner and that when she emerged twenty minutes later she was drunk. What he couldn't understand was how it happened so quickly. She didn't do spirits by choice and he used to wonder if she was on drugs. I'm an ex-student and so have some first-hand experience in the matter.

I told him that it was quite possible that she might be drinking the wine along with liberal helpings of anti-depressants. The truth is we will never know how she got the way she did, only that she did. And when she did she could behave very badly.

The more observant among you may have noticed that I mentioned in the paragraph before the last that I picked my Dad up from around the corner from his house. There's a reason for that. One day I was coming home from market and I got a phone call from Lisa. Beverley was outside my house screaming. I have had to get the family to give me their account of this as obviously I wasn't there. Apparently what happened was that Molly was in the bath and Lisa was sitting on the toilet next to her, taking her make up off with simple make up remover wipes, when they heard someone leaning on a car horn outside the house. Molly was still in the bath so Lisa went and answered the door but because she didn't have her glasses on she didn't instantly recognise the person outside, then the penny dropped and she said "Beverley?"

Beverley was standing outside drunk, she said to Lisa:

"I think we need to talk". She was in tears.

"About what?" replied Lisa.

"Talk about us". slurred Beverley, still crying.

It was at this point that Molly, who had heard Beverley's voice and so ejected herself from the bath sharpish emerged at the front door and said

"What are you doing here Beverley?"

It was then that Beverley flipped. I am a lucky man; I have a beautiful family. I know we all think our kids are pretty and smart but Molly does bear more than a passing resemblance to a young Julia Roberts, she just does. Unfortunately, Molly's beauty and youth had a more than detrimental effect on Beverley's mood.

"You don't know what is important in life".

Molly laughed and replied incredulously "We don't know what's important in life!"

"No you don't". Beverley emphasised.

Then Lisa looked at Molly. She was still taking her make-up off. To this day she doesn't know why, she says at the time she wasn't in a right frame of mind. Beverley saw the exchanged glance between Lisa and Molly and said.

"Don't look at her, don't look at your daughter. You two princesses' in your ivory tower".

Then Beverley saw 'Marley', despite being skint we had not long ago acquired a second hand Mini Countyman who Lisa had christened Marley. The sight of said car made Beverley even more angry.

"What the fuck is that?" exclaimed Beverley.

"It's not mine". Lisa lied.

"I can't fucking believe that you've got a new fucking car". Obviously not the most convincing lie in the world. Beverley then sarcastically referred to the fact that Lisa was still wiping her face with simple wipes by saying: "Oh yeah your beautiful, I'm beautiful". The latter statement referring to herself.

"Just go home Beverley". said Moll.

"Don't talk to me". replied Beverley and then said "You don't know, your grandad pays for everything in here, your dad is a useless Cunt". Marginally insulting. Then she called Molly 'an ugly little bitch'. Massively insulting and also not true.

"Mum just shut the door". Molly said to Lisa and the two of them went in and locked the door.

At this point Beverley started banging on the door shouting "Open the door, open the fucking door".

Molly turned to Lisa and said "Right mum call the police".

"What's the number?" replied Lisa, clearly reeling from the whole debacle.

"999 mum".

"It's like your dad's step-mum, really ring the police?" replied Lisa

"Yes!" replied Molly with conviction.

Lisa rung the police and explained the situation while Beverley was banging and crashing about outside. Then Beverley drove off. However, before she drove off there was a strange scraping noise and a loud thud. She had picked up the milk churn that lived by the front door and dumped it on the roof of the car.

While all of this was going on I was only ten minutes away from the house. I drove home as quickly as I could. My intention was to block the driveway with the van. Lisa had called the police and I hoped that if I blocked Beverley in then when the police turned up and breathalysed her then she would be done for drunk driving. The amount that she must of had could have sent her to prison. You live in hope. As it was by the time I got there she had driven off. The police arrived and took statements from Lisa and Molly and inspected the damage done to the car. In all honesty all that was left was a tiny ding in the roof but it turns out that this was all that was necessary for them to bring a case of criminal damage. We wanted the police to arrest her there and then but due of the constraints on police time this wasn't possible. Instead some months later Beverley was arrested and cautioned. She admitted the offence but was in no way reticent. She turned up at my house out of the blue and screamed at my wife and daughter and then damaged my car but she didn't believe that she has done anything wrong. I don't know whether she is so insensitive that she can't see the emotional damage that she does or that she knows what she is doing but would rather pretend that she was right than admit that she was drunk and out of control. Perhaps she does believe that she was right but that just makes her a fucking idiot. All I know is that I now have what is called a red flag on my house which means that if she does it again the police will have a squad car there in five minutes.

The day after I went round to talk to Beverley. At the time of it happening Lisa had said that she thought that it was better that I didn't talk to her but on the second day she changed her mind. She also kind of had the hump with me because she couldn't understand how I could be fine with the fact that someone had insulted his wife and daughter and I just sat there and did nothing. Firstly, she told me not to do anything. Secondly I don't like confrontation, no one does. Particularly if that confrontation is with an out of control drunk whose mood and attitude directly effects the situation of my rather poorly father. Nevertheless Lisa was right, no one has the right to behave the way she did and just get away with it. Still I have to be honest I was not looking forward to this, not least because, thirdly, I had tried it once before.

Ch. 5 Obscene Telephone Caller

One evening, long before milk churn gate we got a telephone call. It was Beverley. This was not unusual; in fact it had become a relatively common occurrence. Beverley would ring late in the evening. She would go into their bedroom so that Dad couldn't hear her and inevitably she would be drunk. I would then get the usual drunken tirade of: 'Your dads going to die; he's leaving me; I don't know what I am going to do; it's so unfair' etc etc. Just what you need to hear while watching your father die of cancer. You may ask 'if you knew what was going to happen why did you answer the phone?' The answer is simple: you fear that the one time that you don't pick up the phone is the one time that something is seriously wrong and that if you had picked up the phone you could have done something about it. Despite the rhetoric always being the same I tried to be supportive by saying that I know he is going to die but that we have to stay strong for dad's sake and you never know miracles do happen. I did this partly to raise her spirits for Dad's sake, but mainly just to try to keep her calm and get her off the phone as quickly as possible. Drunk talk is the worst. Pissed people just like the sound of their own voice and they don't care what nonsense they talk as long as there is someone to listen. If you are drunk and you want someone to talk to find someone else who's drunk, they have them in pubs and on street corners all over London. I say I was always supportive; I was for the first half a dozen phone calls or so. Near the end I just chose to ignore them. Wonderful thing caller ID. As big Dave said to me: "You'll

soon find out soon enough if something is seriously wrong."
On this particular night the phone went and Beverley's
number came up. I elected to ignore it as I knew the old
routine but Lisa who was becoming a bit tired of the late night
drunken calls decided that she would call her back. I think
she did this in the hope that if Beverley thought in the future
she would get Lisa on the other side of the phone she would
be less likely to call. The conversation went like this.

"Beverley what's going on, is everything alright, is Bob
alright?"

"Yes, yes he's alright".

"Why are you ringing Beverley?"

"He's going to die". she wailed.

"I know he's not well Bev but constantly dwelling on the fact
isn't helping anyone".

"No one understands what it's like".

"I'm not disputing what you are saying Bev but you've got to
understand that Peter's got this with both his parents, it's
incredibly difficult for him at the moment". Beverley's
response was unusual.

"Don't fucking patronise me". she said. Lisa wasn't.

"I'm not patronising you I'm just telling you that it's really hard for Peter as both his parents are going through the same thing".

"It's alright for you sitting over there in your big barn". the conversation had shifted from my Dad's illness to Beverley's real issue but I'll come on to that in a bit.

"What's that got to do with it?" said LIsa.

"You need to get off of your arse and get a job". Beverley was scatter gunning now.

"Beverley this isn't about me this is about Bob". said Lisa but by now she was stuck in a drunken conversation loop.

"He's going to die; he's going to die".

Now I don't know if it is because Lisa was involved, or because I knew that that was what my Dad had to cope with or simply because I wanted an end to this ridiculous conversation but I lost my temper. I grabbed the phone from Lisa and shouted at Beverley:

"Beverley I've had enough, don't ever call this fucking house again". and slammed the phone down. I thought that would be a good thing. I thought that it would put Beverley in her place and that that would be the end of the drunken telephone conversations. I thought wrong. The phone then repeatedly rang (we didn't answer it this time) and we got various drunken answer phone messages saying that we couldn't get rid of her that easily and that she was just going to carry on ringing until we answered and then eventually it stopped. It stopped because I unplugged the phone. Surely that was the end of it.

As the following days passed by Lisa was becoming more and more annoyed at my inaction. To be honest I didn't want to face Beverley, I couldn't see the point. She was completely drunk, would remember nothing of the conversation and in her mind she would be right. Beverley was not the kind of person who would wake up sober in the morning and think 'oh my god what have I done'. She is the kind of drunk who would replay the previous nights' events and change them into a way in which in her mind it was us in the wrong. Still I knew that I would have to face her. I had to, to show LIsa that I would. I elected to do it on the following Sunday morning, I had always gone round on Sunday mornings since a previous drunken phone call during which Beverley accused me of not having enough to do with my Dad. This was rather rich coming from the woman who had done a pretty good job of isolating him from his only grandchild and the rest of the family but I thought 'okay, fair enough' and every Sunday I used to pop around for coffee. I also knew that if I turned up out of the blue there was a good possibility that she would be drunk and If I phoned to say that I was coming round she would know why I was coming and she would go out. Sunday's were usually quite convivial but this Sunday was going to be somewhat different. I went round and had a coffee and after we had done the usual pleasantries I said "Beverley we have to talk".

Now I wasn't shitty. I explained to her that her drinking had got out of control and that she couldn't talk to

149

anyone, especially my wife the way that she did, but I went on to try to be positive. I said that there was still plenty of time left for the two of them and that they had plenty of money and there was still so much they could do to enjoy their life. If Beverley could only get herself under control. After I had said my piece there was a slight pause and my Dad said "I agree with Peter." I thought 'that comment's going to cost you'. Sure enough she denied all of it. She said that what actually happened was that Lisa had called her that night to tell her that her husband, my Dad, was going to die. That is what she had told my Dad had happened and in return he asked me: "Is that right? Did Lisa phone Bev." You see what I was up against? Why on earth would Lisa call Beverley, who she neither liked nor talked to, late one night to tell her that her husband was going to die?

There is a principle in philosophy called Occam's razor. It's a problem solving principle. It states that among competing hypotheses, the one with the fewest assumptions should be selected. In a nutshell what that means is that the most likely explanation is usually the correct one. So with this in mind why did Dad even have to ask the question? Again the answer is simple: Because he had to live with her, that's why. He had to at least show some form of outward solidarity, otherwise Beverley would just accuse him of taking my side and not supporting her which she would then probably use as an excuse to start drinking. I left knowing that I had achieved absolutely nothing and that after agreeing with me, Dad was now in for a really shitty afternoon.

This is why I was not looking forward to having the conversation a second time. I had tried being reasonable and got nowhere but being the soft person that I am I still didn't want to give up hope. As I drove around to their house I wondered if there was any way that I could try to get through to her. I was also well aware that what was required of me was that I had to tear a strip off of her. As it was this time she made it really easy for me. I knocked on the door on that Wednesday night and when Beverley answered the door I could tell instantly that she was drunk again. Strangely I didn't expect this. Dad had always led me to believe that she wasn't drunk all of the time and that if she had a drink one day she wouldn't have one the next. This clearly wasn't true. Her attitude was one of pure arrogance I didn't even get a chance to start talking. Beverley went straight into a tirade saying that she didn't care that we had called the police on her, that there was no real damage to the car and that she had gone round to talk to Lisa and Molly but instead of talking to her they had been laughing at her and put their fingers up at her. More unbelievable drunken nonsense. Trying to reason with someone totally unreasonable is tiring and to have to stand there when they are constantly talking bollocks insulting my family was enough to make me lose my temper.

I do have a temper but It's well buried as well it should be after years of working on the market. I have had to build up an armour to protect myself from the stupid things that customers say and do. I have pat answers for most of the ridiculous things that they come out with and ways of fielding and diffusing difficult situations but they can still get under the armour. The last time I lost my rag on the market was

151

when one particular punter came up to me with a packet of boxer shorts and said "I could have nicked these but I didn't, so you have to give me them cheaper". He exited the stall very quickly after that with me right behind him screaming words that none of the women on my stall should ever have to hear. The quickest way to get me to lose my temper is to insult someone near to me. The second she accused Lisa and Molly of giving her the V sign (which I knew to be a lie, I know how they work) I told her in no uncertain terms and with the use of colourful language that she was a drunken worthless human being and that she was never to come anywhere near my family again. That was the last time I saw Beverley for a long time. It was also the last time I picked Dad up from in front of his house. Needless to say I no longer visited them on a Sunday morning. I wonder if she engineered it that way.

I should point out that aside from being mental there was a reason why Beverley hated Lisa so much. Lisa had the life that she had hoped to steal and they were partly financing it. When I first took over the business from my Dad it was doing rather well. This was more than in part down to me. I had finished college massively over qualified and with a girlfriend (now my wife) who I was not prepared to expose to the three more years of enduring poverty so that I could get the qualification I needed to have any chance of lecturing. I was qualified as an administrator despite being the worst administrator in the world. The director of the only company I ever worked for (I had to do a year's work experience as part of my degree) said that they would give me a shining reference in anything I wanted to do in my later life, as long as it was not in administration. The only other thing that I really knew how to do was market trade so it was all of a bit of a fait accompli really.

Dad set me up in a van on various home counties markets like Chesham and St Neots. Nice little market towns within pleasant surroundings and polite customers that didn't spend very much money. I asked once why he let me carry on with it, "you were cheap" he replied. The thing is that despite it being easy I wasn't happy, I knew that markets could take big money, I had grown up with ones that did and so I looked elsewhere. More specifically I went to London. Within a year of going to work for my Dad I had established a round of London markets and the figures had gone through the roof.

For a while I was happy. I went to work and took good money, the wages were fine and I had no hassles. That was the way it was until one day I booked to take Lisa to Brighton for the weekend. I was working on the Saturday and so we would set off after I got back from work. However, on the way home from work Friday the van started making some very strange noises. I drove it straight round to Stuart the mechanic who informed me in no uncertain terms that that van was going nowhere. Good news for me I could have a lie in on Saturday morning and we could still be down to Brighton for lunchtime.

We set off for Brighton in the morning and halfway through the journey we stopped at services. Lisa was pregnant with Molly at the time and a toilet break was necessary. As Lisa was relieving herself I thought I would ring home and see how things were. My Mum answered.

"Hello mum". I said.

"Your dad's not happy with you". she said. You'll notice two things from this opener. Firstly, no hello. Why do people do that. If you've got the hump at least start with a pleasantry before jumping into an attack. Secondly apparently it was my Dad who was not happy with me, not her. No it wasn't. She wanted to have a go and it was easy to use Dad as an excuse. I've got the hump now.

"Why?" I said.

"Because of the van".

"How's that my fault?" I replied.

"You should have known".

I found this statement somewhat puzzling.

"How am I supposed to know mum? I'm not a mechanic".

"Stuart said it must have been making a noise for ages".

Well it wasn't. Why would I drive a van that was making funny noises? All that would happen is that it would break down on the way home, I would have to wait for the AA who would come out and say that they couldn't fix it, they would then send a recovery truck and the guy would tell me that he couldn't lift it because the van was overloaded (scumbag market traders, we all drive overloaded vans) I would offer him a drink to take it and I would eventually make it home two hours late. Alternatively, I could say that the van was making funny noises and get the day off on full pay. Occam's razor, what would you do? I will admit there have been times when I have been driving in my own van and it has started to make funny noises when I have tried to ignore it in the hope that it goes away but that I only because I was poor and didn't want to pay the mechanics bill for the repair. You just tell yourself that it has always sounded like that. Or turn the radio up. By the time I finished the conversation I had been transformed from 'happily looking forward to my weekend break away' to 'I'm fed up now, why do they have to ruin everything'. My resentment grew until the point over Lunch when I said to Lisa "I don't need this grief; I could do this on my own." By the end of lunch, I had made plans to. I am like that. I'm like that sheep in the Monty Python sketch, once I get an idea into my head there's no stopping it.

155

That is how I came to be a self-employed market trader. I still bought gear off of my Dad and he earned off of me on the wholesale so he still made money but I no longer gave him any problems, not that I ever really gave him any problems anyway and I made a ton of money by taking our gear to the poorest areas of London. Looking back the sensible thing to do with all of this extra cash would have been to consolidate. Get a little house and pay off the mortgage. Make plans for the future. We didn't. We spunked it. We went for weekends away. We brought expensive clothes. There were always huge bunches of flowers around the house. After all, if I was doing this well now, think how well I would be doing in a few years' time. Then things started to go wrong.

Did you hear the one about the accountant and the market trader?

An accountant and a market trader go out for lunch and the market trader says to the account:

"What would you do if you won the lottery?" The accountant replies:

"Being an accountant and knowing that the odds of me winning are so astronomical, I wouldn't do the lottery. However, let's say hypothetically that I did and let's say that I won. I would have a huge mansion house, a fleet of the finest cars, the most expensive clothes, exotic holidays, lavish parties, and when the money is gone, it's gone".

"Not me" replies the market trader "It wouldn't change my life one bit. I would still be up at four o'clock every morning, work eighteen hour days seven days a week – and when the money's gone, it's gone".

Tell that joke to a member of the pubic and you might get a laugh, tell it to a market trader and they just nod. Like progress my poverty didn't happen overnight. If you drop a frog into a pan of boiling water it will jump straight out, if you drop a frog into a pan of cold water and then slowly bring it to the boil it will sit there until it is cooked. I was a bit like that. The figures started to fall and instead of doing something about it I started making excuses. A bad day here and there which you initially put down to the weather, or the fact that it's the end of the month so no one had been paid, or it's Eid so some of our customers are resting, or the fact that there's a road closed in town, or the tube strike. Believe me I am a master at this. My next book is going to be called 'One hundred and one excuses for why I am having a crap day'. I have got it sorted into chapters. My favourite chapter is 'Excuses that you can only use once in your life time'. I was standing on East Street one day, and in fairness it wasn't that bad when a trader I didn't know sidled up to me and I could tell from his body language what was coming.

"How's your day?" He said. I decided to play along.

"Bit slow". I replied. "What do you put it down to?"

"We'll it's the solar eclipse ain't it". and I thought I will never be able to use that excuse again.

Slowly but surely the bad days became all too frequent and the money I was taking decreased. Problem was my spending didn't. I took stock from my father on tick, used the money to finance my lifestyle and then took more stock on tick. I know that I shouldn't have done this but I always assumed that could turn it around and that I would eventually be able to trade my way out of it. Dad would always do his best to help me but I just couldn't seem to get ahead. There I was living in a converted barn that has a living room so big that you could land a plane in it and there was Beverley in the small one-bedroom place around the corner while all of the time I owed them a pile of money. It's no wonder that she had the hump.

On top of all of this Lisa didn't work. She had given up her job as a secretary to have Molly and at first there was no need for her to go back, I made enough money for the both of us. When things started to get tough we talked about the idea of her returning to work. Problem was that Lisa would only be on a basic wage and once you take into account the tax benefits we would lose the difference to our income would be negligible. Plus, I have to confess I liked having Lisa at home. For most of my childhood either my Mum or my Grandma were at home most of the time and I think for a child this is a good thing. To know that there is constantly a parent on call is reassuring. You may be in school but you know that if you suddenly get sick they would be there within twenty minutes; it makes you feel safe. The problem was that while I owed my Dad for stock I was making that decision with someone else's money. Then there was Molly. Beverley had chosen to inhabit my mother's life but that was one part of it that she would never have. She would never have children with Dad, he didn't want any more children and besides he had had the snip. I have often wondered what it would have been like if he hadn't and they had decided to have a family. What is it like to find out aged thirty that you are no longer going to be an only child and that you are in fact going to get a sibling who is younger than your own kid. Must be a very strange place to be. I have to confess that I am pleased that there is one part of my Mum's life that Beverley could never have. The joke is if she had only been different she could have been like a third grandparent to Moll but they didn't want to be grandparents. They wanted to be like a young single couple and so baggage like an existing family didn't enter the equation. At birthdays Dad used to say to me "You get her whatever you like and I'll knock the money off your bill". He would be very generous with the amounts as he would admit that he didn't do anything with her for the rest of the time. "I'm a crap grandparent" he used to say. I would tell him that it didn't matter, that Molly had plenty of support from us and Lisa's family but to be honest actually it did matter. As time went by Molly blossomed from a little dot into a beautiful young woman right in front of Beverley's eyes and so the resentment grew.

Lisa says that she totally understands the way that Beverley feels. She says that if she was living in a one-bedroom house while some other woman who owed her a pile of money was living in a castle round the corner she would resent her too but as Lisa points out she never actually did

159

anything wrong, all she did was stay at home and look after our daughter. If the blame rests with anyone it should rest with me. I should have managed our money better. I should never have taken out all those credit cards with twelve months zero percent interest thinking 'Look at these idiots they're giving me ten grand to play with for free. It's not a problem once the twelve months runs out I'll just transfer the balance to another card'. Till the zero interest cards ran out and I was left with one hundred K's worth of debt. I should have known better, there's is no such thing as a free loan. Even if you borrow money off of your friends or family you are essentially selling some of your freedom because then they have a say in the way that you lead your life. "They haven't paid us back and yet they are booking a holiday" or "She still owes me twenty quid and she's just been out shoe shopping" and they have a point. If you can afford luxuries, you can afford to pay them back. Of course some people will lend you money graciously and say nothing but that doesn't mean that at the end of the day you are taking the piss out of them and don't think that they don't know it. The fact that we owed so much while our life was better than hers ate away at Beverley until she could contain it no longer and I don't blame her for this. What I object to was her choice of target, it was all aimed at Lisa when in truth it was all my fault. The thing is you don't want to blame your own son. No it couldn't be him that fucked up it must have been someone else. It doesn't take a genius to work out who the closest soft target would be.

I never took the fact that I owed my Dad money lightly. Many times I thought about selling my house and moving into rented just to clear my debts. Problem was that I couldn't sell the house to pay them back because of the fall in the housing market that had happened whilst living my champagne life on my beer income. Also I didn't want to make the same mistake that my father had. My friend Paul Corner's, best man Darren's dad once told me "Buy the best house that you can, even if it's a massive stretch and do everything that you can to keep hold of it, in the long run you won't regret it." Way things are starting to pan out I believe that he was right. Property prices may fluctuate but ultimately they only go one way. To be honest even if I could have why would I? My Dad was dying. I would be selling my house to give the money to the woman who split up my parent's marriage and was somewhat responsible for why my father never saw his only granddaughter so that she could drink it. Not an attractive prospect. I say somewhat responsible but to be honest Dad was never bothered about Moll. Neither of my parents were. I want to believe that if they had stayed together and as Molly became more of an adult they would have both warmed to her but I will never know. In truth at any time during his relationship with Beverley he could have put his foot down and said that he was going to see his granddaughter but he never did. Dad used to say to me "I'm a crap grandfather." Lisa used to say to me "that's not an excuse."

Ch.7 Will to power

As a result of the increasing rift between us I saw less and less of my Dad. I started to hang on to any reason I could just to see him but I tended to be thwarted at each turn. He became concerned about the fact that the cancer treatment was making him weak. Although not a big man, I used to joke in the summer that he was browner and thinner than Ghandi, he was surprisingly strong. It's a useful trait to have as a market trader as you do spend a lot of your time unloading heavy boxes. It is also one that you take for granted. I am lucky enough to inherit some of his strength. If there is ever anything that needs moving I will always try to move it on my own. If someone ever says 'I'll give you a hand with that' my reply is 'no, I'm alright' and then do my best to shift it, even at the risk of giving myself a bloody hernia. I was lucky to be born strong but also unlucky enough to have become vain. Recently I started to get shooting pains down my arms when loading up the van. It is only at that point that you realise what you actually have and then the fear of losing it sets in. It's the same with everything, eyesight, hair, the ability to tie your shoes. The thing is you can compensate for some things. Glasses a wig and slip-ons, it's a good look. One thing you can't compensate for is the inability to control your body. A side effect of the brain cancer meant Dad had begun to have epileptic fits. It first happened when Dad and Beverley had gone away with friends for Christmas. They were having a perfectly lovely time until Dad had gone into the main dining room. He said he thought that it was the subtle pulsing of the ceiling tube lights that did it. He started to shake and so left the dining room for the hallway and that is where he had his first full on fit. I asked him what it was like and he said "It's weird. You command your body to stop but it just keeps moving and there is nothing that you can do about it." Dad never complained about any of his illness but he told me that the inability to control your body is terrifying. The onset of epileptic fits also meant that he couldn't drive which made him even more dependent on my step-mum. So that's all good.

To combat the weakness in his body Dad decided that he would like to go to the gym and I suggested that we could go to the gym together. I was free on Monday mornings and I would take him. It would also do me a favour as it would help me get back in shape and I kind of know what I am doing. I joked that I could be his personal trainer. I picked him up on the Monday morning (round the corner from his house) and we headed off into town. Now gym's fit into two different categories: There are the modern gyms where everything is shiny and chrome and they have banks of running machines all lined up in a row facing large television screens that show the news and MTV. Gyms that have clean weight stations into which you can insert a USB stick and track your progress via the app on your iPhone. Gyms where women turn up in matching Lyrica and brightly coloured trainers with full faces of makeup. Then there are the other sort of gyms. Blokes gyms. Gyms that smell of sweat. Gyms where all of the weights and machines look like they have been made out of reclaimed scrap metal from a railway yard. Gyms where the carpet is threadbare in places and there is a large counter behind which sits an incredibly muscularly man in a vest who is covered in tattoos and who will sell you large plastic containers of 'weight gain' and presumably steroids from under the counter. We went to the second type for three reasons: It was quiet during the day; you don't need a contract and it was cheap.

Dad liked cheap. He was always very generous with others but mean with himself. He had had quite a hard upbringing and so could never see the value in certain things. The clothes he wore all came from the market. He simply couldn't work out why you would pay twenty pounds over the odds for a black t shirt just because it had a tick on it. He made a flask of coffee every morning rather than paying the seventy pence they charged at the tea waggon. Like I say he wasn't mean, if we ever went out for a meal he would always pay for everything and tell us to order whatever we wanted regardless of price. It was just some things he just couldn't see. This gym suited him fine. We went around the machines and I showed him how they worked. I set him on a programme that was not too intensive but that would make him feel like he was making progress. Most of all I was with him so that if anything untoward (like him having a fit) happened I would be there to take care of him. It was fun. Fun that lasted two weeks. Then Dad said that Beverley also wanted to get fit so they were going to go together instead. I knew what she was doing and so did he but he was stuck. They went to the gym together for three weeks and then it stopped.

As I said from the very beginning they had set themselves up in a separate life. Kind of a 'you and me against the world' situation. I personally think that this is a really bad idea. I can't help but wonder how much better we could do as a race if we acted more like ants, if we actually pulled together rather than just being a collection of individuals who don't murder and steal purely because they are afraid of the consequences. Think about how much better things could be if the first thought that entered our minds was: 'What can I do for you?" Instead of: "What's in it for me?" Oh well. As it is being totally independent is all well and good when you are healthy but when you are ill you need support and despite the set-up, that support was offered. I constantly offered our help and so did Lisa but it was rarely accepted. I believe that if Dad did ever take us up on our offers the prospect of "what are you going to them for?" would have been too much to bear and so he elected to do many things on his own, which for a man in his condition was really not a good idea. Even before the falling out it was difficult. When Dad was undergoing his second bout of treatment for his lungs at Stoke Mandeville Hospital, me and Beverley were talking. I knew she was mental and I knew she was drunk but she hadn't abused my family so I played the game for the sake of my Dad. He was in hospital and I was going to see him so in the interests of helping I offered to take her. It was clear when I picked her up that she had been on the sauce and I had to listen to how she was incredibly independent one moment and how she couldn't survive without him the next for the entire trip. The problem with some drunks is that they think that you can't tell that they are drunk, they think they get away with it. They don't. Like poker players they have tells. An eye goes funny or they play with their hair and you know they've gone again. Dad knew instantly, he knew her too well. He told me in the hospital, when she went to the toilet, that he knew that she was drunk. He said "she can't even stay sober when she comes and visit me". Then he said that he was concerned about how he would get out of hospital. Beverley was supposed to come and pick him up the following day but she had a tendency to drink too much and pass out. Even if she didn't pass out there was still the distinct possibility she would still be driving drunk. I told him that it wasn't a problem as all he had to do was call Lisa and she would come and get him. I said I would even take the day off work to come and get him although I knew that this would never wash because there was no way that Dad would ever want me to take a day off of work. He never did call. I found out a week later that after overcoming a major operation he did the hour journey home on his own in a taxi.

He would be the first to admit it, he had created his own life. Although he had helped plenty of people along the way if you set yourself up as a couple against the world you set yourself away from help and as Beverley's drinking became worse Dad did things more and more independently. He was no longer allowed to drive, so he took to walking to the warehouse which was a good hours shuffle away. When I asked him why he didn't just call Lisa he would say that he liked the exercise. That was how we came to spend a Bank Holiday together.

I am always up before the rest of the family; my body clock goes off. It was a bank holiday Monday and I was

166

standing in the front room playing guitar badly. I looked out of my window and saw Dad coming up the drive. My initially reaction was that of happiness 'oh look dad's here'. Then I noticed the blood pouring from his mouth. I brought him in and sat him at the kitchen table. He had decided to get himself out of the house for a while so had begun the walk to the warehouse where he would have a tidy up. As he came through the village he had tripped on a paving stone, fallen and knocked his front tooth out. I tried to stop the bleeding but it wasn't happening and so the two of us took a trip to the accident and emergency department of the Luton and Dunstable Hospital. There is a point in our relationship with our parents where they become the child and you become the adult. Sitting with him in the waiting room he just kept repeating how sorry he was and how stupid he had been and I just kept reassuring him that it wasn't a problem and that accidents happen every day. I didn't want him to become the child, not for my sake but for his, we all have our pride. We spent the Monday morning at A and E who patched him up and told him that he needed a new tooth. I told him that that wasn't going to be cheap and that he should get himself to my dentist in Dunstable who was NHS, god knows he'd paid enough tax in this life. He didn't. He went private and for the same job the tooth cost him over two grand. I genuinely think he did it to punish himself.

This was a telling sign as Dad was not that kind of guy. He was always optimistic. If things were good he would spend his money and enjoy it, if things were bad, he would work hard and cut this cloth accordingly. Life for him was always good. But I was starting to notice a change in him.

167

Not in his physical condition but in the very nature of his soul. Our will has a dramatic effect on our lives. There is a fantastic book called 'The Man Who Mistook His Wife for a Hat'. It's about neurological disorders. In the book there is a study of a man who through some kind of fencing accident damaged a part of his brain that controlled will. As a result, he lost his will to do anything. He felt no compulsion to get dressed, to move or even to eat. A strange side effect of the accident was that the objects around him started to disappear. He could no longer see certain pieces of furniture or cars parked in the street and as a result would walk right into them. The prevailing school of thought of why this happened is that our brain only actually sees the world around us because it is in the way. Once it ceases to be perceived as an obstacle then there is no need to see it at all and so it disappears. Reality is an illusion; albeit a very persistent one. Even if this isn't the case I think it is a generally accepted truth that our chances of survival are strongly linked to our will to survive. Beverley behaviour was wearing my Dad down and he was coming to accept it. He once said to me "What's the matter with me son, I once ran a million-pound business and now look at me, I can't stand up to a drunken woman." My Dad was starting to lose the will to live.

It was inevitable that things would eventually come to a head between Dad and Beverley. He reached the point that he just couldn't put up with it any longer and I got the phone call to come and get him. I met him around the corner from his house. He was slightly stooped but defiant carrying a small holdall of clothes. He told me that her behaviour was getting worse to the stage that there were no longer any good days and that he just couldn't live with her any longer. I took him to mine where he stayed for dinner and the night. I told him that he was welcome to stay with me for as long as he wanted but he was all too well aware that anyone who comes to stay in your house, no matter how close they are to you, are an imposition and he would never do that. Besides ultimately he wanted independence and his own place, this was a long term plan. For the short term he had decided to move to Bellows Mill while he looked for somewhere to rent.

Having Dad in Bellows Mill gave me an enormous sense of Deja vu. He was now in exactly the same situation that Mum had been in before her operation. I would pop in in the evening, on my way home from work and in the mornings, on my days off, to see how he was. He said that he was happy to be away from the madness and that he was considering not renting and staying there indefinitely. I was aware of the fact that he was pretty much stuck in there on his own all day long and so I suggested that he came to work with me a couple of days a week. He loved work and it would get him away from the same four walls. It also meant that I would get to spend more time with my Dad. We worked well together, we always had. He made suggestions of how I should rearrange my business and I took them. Why wouldn't I, it made him happy and besides, he was good at what he did.

Then after a while his resolve started to wane and again I understand this. My marriage like most has not been without it's up and downs. There have been rows where the situation became so untenable that I have moved out (into Belllows Mill, in case you hadn't guessed) resolute that that was the end of it and that I would put up with it no longer but then time passes. You come to reflect on your actions and you start to think 'was it all their fault? Perhaps I was being unreasonable'. In the end even if you believe that it is not your fault if you love someone you will go back because you love them no matter how much of a nightmare they might be. They say that love is blind, can't see it myself.

Dad had been talking to Beverley on the phone. She had been sober and she missed him. They had arranged to see each other again. She came to visit him in his new place at the mill and again she had been sober. She had told him that she had missed him and that she was sorry. She wanted him to come back and she was going to go to Alcoholics Anonymous and get professional help. He meant that much to her that she was going to stop drinking altogether. He told me that he had decided to go back but that if she started drinking again he was going to move straight back into Bellows Mill and this time he wouldn't go back. Now let's play a game. Can you spot how many lies were told in this paragraph?

She was back on the booze part time within a week and back on it properly within two. Dad didn't move out. Whether it was because he felt silly or that even drunk he found that some company is better than no company at all I don't know. I think that he had just resigned himself to it being his lot in life. I also think that the company you keep has to get pretty bad before you leave. I have a friend who I call Dave the Crisps. I told you we all have nick names. He is a devoted father, phenomenal guitarist and my ex next door neighbour on Hoxton market. He is also the nicest man I have ever met. He is no longer a market trader because unlike me he finished the knowledge and is now a black cab driver. Just before 'passing out' he found out that his wife was having an affair with her boss. He also found out that she had previously slept with his brother. They still live together. They no longer share a bed; he has changed the front sitting room into a bedroom. They don't even really talk anymore. I can't see how anyone can do that. I can't see how you can stay with someone who you loved, who then betrayed your trust so badly. I asked him why he stayed and said: "don't tell me it is for the sake of the kids because you know that doesn't work". He explained that it wasn't for the sake of the kids but that he loved his kids, they were everything to him and he wanted to see every moment of them growing up. Something that would be denied to him if he left, denied through no fault of his own. He also said that he had worked hard to pay for the house and why should he give half of it to "that bitch". I believe everything he says to be true. There is also a separate possible explanation. When you love someone it doesn't matter how badly they behave because at the end of the day you still love them and want to be with them despite what they have become. This may not be true for Dave but I think that it was true for Dad.

Ch.9 Back to hospital

As part of one of his routine check-ups Dad had had a cat scan and they discovered another tumour on his brain. This meant another operation which to some might have been a big deal but when you spend your life having brain operations it becomes part of the old routine. The amount that he had had they could have installed a zip. No one was worried as the operation was a small affair and the whole thing would be relatively straight forward. Despite this we had a meeting up the warehouse the Monday before he went in. As far as I was concerned we were just going up for our usual Monday slot up the warehouse. I would pick him up and he could unload about all of Beverley's recent antic's on the way up to the yard. Then we would move a few boxes around, have a powdered cappuccino in a Styrofoam cup, all of the proper mugs were dirty because none of us could ever be bothered to wash them up, play 'pop master' and then I would take him home. This particular Monday he had a folder with him. The folder contained various different invoices. It was so that he could show me exactly who owed him what and where. To be honest I wasn't really listening. Talking about money is a crass subject at the best of times but especially when it is related to ill health. I already knew that when Dad died the house and all of the money would all go to Beverley. She was his wife and would need the money to support her once he was gone, particularly as she was much younger than him. Fair enough. I was to inherit the business. This basically meant that I would inherit all the debts of the people who owed him money, the largest of which was mine. I kind of got my inheritance while my father was still alive which is fine because it meant that I got it when I most needed it. The other reason that I wasn't listening was because it was just a routine operation. The surgeons said he could have years yet. I said to him "You don't have to tell me all this, we'll be back here next week trying to remember who sang 'Tarzan Boy'". He replied, "I know, I just feel better in my own head knowing that it's all straight".

As it was the operation did go well and he telephoned me the evening of the next day to say that he felt better than ever. I would say that he was high on the drug of life but to be honest it was more likely to be diazepam. They would keep him in for a couple of days and then he would be free to come home and this time he was coming home to me. Soon after the operation I had gone to visit Dad in hospital. He had told Beverley that she was not to visit him. Her drinking was out of control and on her first visit she had made a scene in the ward so he had told her to stay away. Me and Dad had had a meeting with the consultant who had explained that when Dad was discharged he would need constant care. He was far from being an invalid, he seemed okay but he would require bed rest and someone there at all times in case there were any complications. I had told the consultant that my step-mum spent half her life drunk and the other half asleep and that we were more than happy to have him. We all agreed that this would be the best way forward. I hoped that this could actually be his first proper step on his road to independence, even if this hope was somewhat hope over experience. Dad was due to come out in a couple of days. I had offered to take

174

the day off work but of course he said no. After all this is the man went to work on the morning of my Uncles wedding. It wouldn't have been so bad but he was best man. It's like I said, my Dad was old school, you didn't miss work. We agreed that I would come and pick him up when I finished work. Wilsden to Eustons not that far, I could pick him up and have him home in time for tea. Lisa bought steaks, he loved a good steak.

In fact, that is one of Lisa's fondest memories of my Dad. There was a time when they were playing estate agents in Spain that Dad had to fly to England to sign some documents. He was only in the country for two days with an overnight stop and would be flying in and out on his own. I asked him for dinner and Lisa brought steak. It was a warm summers evening and we decided to do a barbeque. We sat out the back, the garden in full bloom, steak on the barbeque and Lisa's iPod on the stereo. My wife is like that. She doesn't like my music (gingly gangly, student wanker, shoe stairer bands) and thinks her music (mainly dance music) is great and everybody loves it. I have tried to point out that she is wrong but she is having none of it. She also gets the hump when I play my music so for the sake of a quiet life I let her dominate the stereo. This only goes to reinforce her belief that everyone likes her music so it's kind of counterproductive really. Oh well.

We finished dinner and I went inside for a bath leaving Lisa and Dad out in the garden. It was then that on random shuffle Fleetwood Mac came on. Dad didn't know that Lisa was a fan, of course he didn't, we never spent any time together. So Lisa put on Rumours and we sat outside drinking and listening to music beneath the pergola fairy lights on that warm summer evening. In the morning he thanked us as he left for a wonderful time and said that it was the best steak he had ever had. It was at that point that Beverley phoned. She knew that he had been staying with us and she was ringing with some supposed problem in Spain. He finished a really short phone call and turned to us angry and frustrated and said "What's the matter with that woman, can't she ever leave it alone." The joy of the previous night had all been washed away.

We wanted his homecoming to be welcoming so Lisa bought steak. Fresh bedding went on and the flowers went in the room, not that Dad was in any way interested in flowers but it made Lisa feel better. But he didn't come home. I phoned him hoping for a pick up time and he told me that there was a complication. The brain operation had gone well but there was a problem with his breathing and they wanted to keep him in to get it under control. I went up to see him a couple of days later, I wasn't being lapse I just wanted to give him time to recover. Sure enough when I did go to visit I found out that my step-mum had been in. She was still drunk and had been brought in by a friend. At first he had refused to see her but then it became apparent that she would create more trouble if he didn't so they had talked. By my second visit he was already starting to say that it would probably better if he went home with Beverley despite my protests. It was as if he was resigned to a fate that he couldn't escape. To cap it all his breathing was getting worse. I asked him if he was in pain and he said "No, it's uncomfortable but no pain."

He could have handled the pain, what was worse was that he was getting frustrated and bored. Bored with the whole thing. In fact, it is the only time in my life that I ever saw my Dad cry. And that was my fault.

I told him my favourite 'Pause for Thought' story. On Radio 2 in the morning they have this thing, it's a kind of thought for the day. Not that I listen to Radio 2, I listen to 6 music. I'm far too cool for Radio 2 and being an ex-student wanker Radio 6 has saved my sanity because I no longer have to listen to over enthusiastic morning Radio and I also get to hear new songs that I actually like. Although I do listen to Simon Mayo on the way home, he's good. And Ken Bruce for pop master. And Jeremy Vines good too. Okay I do still listen to Radio 2 but I am still cool and trendy, honest.

Anyway on this particular morning the appropriate member of the cloth (the readers are always from one religion or another) told this tale:

There are these two guys in a hospital ward. One of them is recovering from a serious back operation and is totally immobile. All he can do is stare at the ceiling. To keep him entertained the other guy tells him what is going on as he looks out of the window opposite his bed. From the window this guy can see a park and he describes the scenes of children playing on the swings, an old gentlemen and his grandson feeding the ducks. He tells of the two people meeting while they walk their dogs. They become friends and are now meeting every day for longer and longer periods. Perhaps romance is in the air.

177

Then one day the man with the bad back no longer hears from his friend. He asks the nurse what has happened and she explains that sadly the gentlemen in the bed near the window passed away during the night. The man with the bad back is saddened by the loss of his friend but also asks the nurse for a favour. His back was now improving and he asks if it would be possible if he could be moved to the bed by the window. The nurse is puzzled by the request but agrees. The man with the bad back is moved to the new location and looks out of the window. The sight that he is met with is that of a brick wall. He calls the nurse and asks "Where is the park?"

"What park?" comes the reply.

"The man in the bed before me used to tell me stories of what he saw in the park". says the man.

"The man in the bed before you was blind". Replied the nurse.

I can't even tell this story without filling up. Like I said, I'm soft. But I didn't expect my Dad to cry. This is the man who went to the funeral of his Mum and both of his sisters with no outward emotion whatsoever. He was an old fashioned man. He never cooked. He tried to do beans on toast once and nearly blew up the house because he took the lid off of the beans and put the tin straight in the microwave. My Dad came from a time when men were not in touch with their feminine side. A time when men didn't cry. And yet here he

was in front of me welling up. Maybe it was the drugs.
Maybe it was something else.

Ch. 10 The complications had a bit of a complication.

I kept visiting my Dad at his ward in Queens, every time hoping that he would have a discharge date. After all they had done the serious operation to do with his brain, this was just fluid on the lungs, no big deal. I had to time my visits so as not to bump into Beverley. I hadn't seen her since the fateful day when I had gone around to talk to her for the second time. The last thing that Dad needed right now was a row in the hospital. Dad had said that he didn't want to see her but in the state he was in he couldn't have stopped her even if he had wanted to and to be perfectly honest, I think he did want to see her. His breathing was still getting worse. They had put a drain on his lung to take the fluid away and hopefully once it was all removed he could be released. When he got out he was going to go home to Beverley. I guess at the end of the day it was his home. There's no place like it.

It was late in the evening when Beverley called my mobile. I ignored it and she left a message. Dad had been moved to a different hospital. The one that he had been in was a brain one. The new hospital was a lung one. Also Dad had been moved to intensive care. He was now in Euston which is a shorter walk than Queens from the tube. In fact it is bang opposite Euston station, strangely enough. There was also the fact that because it was intensive care you were only allowed one visitor at a time and so there was no chance of bumping into Beverley. All in all, a bit of a boon. I had never been in an intensive care unit before. Walking into one of those places for the first time is both impressive and scary. Before you can go into the ward you first have to get through a set of doors that are controlled by buzzers and key cards. It was a bit like being a contestant on the crystal maze. When you finally get into the ward and walk into the room you are met with banks of equipment, monitors and tubes and a nurse constantly by their side. It is fantastic and terrifying at the same time.

All the way through his treatment my father (the ex Bupa member) had nothing but admiration for the NHS. His treatment had been fantastic, the nurses and doctors were all brilliant. He was even a fan of the food. However, it is only when you get to see an ICU for the first time that you realise just how fantastic the NHS is. It's not just the money that this kind of care must cost. It is the value that they put on a life. They take a person who may be really old and terminal and they throw everything that they possibly can at them to make them better. The NHS is one of the greatest things in our country and I won't have a bad word said about it.

I wasn't there for long. He was wearing an oxygen mask as his breathing had become very bad. He couldn't say more than a couple of words before he would have to put the mask back on again. This whole routine left him feeling frustrated and annoyed and that was not the reason why I was there. My father in law who has spent more than his fair share of time in hospital says that one day he is going to write a book on how to be a good hospital visitor. Turn up at the appropriate time, make an effort with your appearance, don't hang around at meal times and don't outstay your welcome. If he doesn't write it then maybe I should, it might turn out to be a best seller in those little branches of W H Smith that they now have in hospital foyers. On second thoughts perhaps not, I hope I am never in a position where I get to find out what it is like to have regular hospital visitors.

By my second visit his condition had improved dramatically. The plan was that he would spend another couple of days in the ICU and then they would move him to an observation ward before finally sending him home. He was feeling relatively cheerful and he could now manage to get out almost a full paragraph without needing the mask. I filled him in on all of the news that was going on in the outside world. This usually took the form of what we were selling and how the markets were. Some men talk football, we talked markets. Markets and music. From about the age of seven if a song came on my Dad would always say "who sang that?". "Dunno dad". was the reply, how would I know? I was seven. Thing is I soon realised that this game wasn't going away in a hurry so I started paying attention. The next time the song would come on and he said "who sang that?" I would tell him. And what group did she used to sing with? I never got off easily but I learned. I have no idea who won the 1986 FA cup final or who the current Leeds goalie is but I know that Elkie Brooks used to sing in Vinegar Joe with Robert Palmer and that the B side of Splodgenessabounds hit 'Two Pints of Larger and a Packet of Crisps' is 'Simon Templar'.

We talked music until I became a market trader, then we talked markets. The thing about market trading is that it is not a vocation, it is a curse. Not so much a curse, more like one of those diseases that can lie dormant in your body but that never actually goes away. Market trading is like Malaria. Or the Hotel California. You can check out any time you like but you can never leave. I can't count the amount of market traders that I have watched retire only to reappear three months later because they missed it and they didn't know what else to do with their time. If you get two market traders together it is all they will talk about, normally about how quiet trade is at the moment, they can't help it. Honestly if you put twelve market traders in a room and told them that they would be shot if they talked about markets you would have a room full of a dozen dead market traders within the first ten minutes.

Once I had finished filling him in I asked him how he was and I am sorry to say that he was low. His health might have been improving but his spirit was falling. My Dad was always the optimistic kind. He was a doer. If things were going well he was happy, if things weren't going well he would do what it took to turn the situation around but I think that he had reached the point where he could no longer see any way out. He said "I don't know Peter I've kind of done it all, what's the actual point of carrying on?" My immediate reaction was to be encouraging. I jumped in with "Of course there's a point. There's still beer and whisky and sunshine and besides it will soon be Christmas". Not the most inspiring speech that I have ever given. Suffice to say it did not have the desired result. His face dropped. I can't read minds but I think the thought of Christmas filled him with dread. What I should have done is actually addressed the question seriously rather than just throwing pat pleasantries at him. The problem was when he asked me 'what is the point of carrying on?' what I actually wanted to say was "there isn't one dad".

As I left the hospital I thought about what I should have said. Dad's health was on the mend and I had to give him a reason to carry on. Then it came to me, the solution was obvious. Dad was a market trader; in fact he was the market trader. I wanted to give my father a reason to go on and I knew exactly what to do. The next time I saw him his condition had slightly worsened and I set about giving him a reason to live. I said "The last time that I saw you, you asked me what is the point and I thought about it. We haven't brought a Babtex parcel yet". Our friend Colin had told us about a company that he dealt with who brought container loads of clothes from Bangladesh and he said that it had made them a lot of money. I said to Dad "We haven't done that yet dad and if I am going to do it I will need your help". He smiled, he knew what I was doing and it hadn't had the effect that I hoped it would have. Whether it was because my response had been too late or more worryingly he was too far gone I will never know. To make the situation worse, at that point my step-mum walked in.

Ch. 11 What would you do?

I froze. I didn't know what to do. Should I just get up and leave without talking to her? Should I chastise her for her behaviour over the past few months, the time when Dad most needed her help? Should I stay talking to Dad but refusing to acknowledge the fact that she was there? In that moment you only have a split second to make that decision, a decision that would ultimately affect the way things went forward from that point onwards. She looked straight at me, she looked nervous and intrepid fearing my response. I looked straight at her and said "Hello Bev".

It was one of those About Schmidt moments. What you imagine you would do, you don't. For many reasons. It was only going one way, my Dad was dying and she was inextricably linked to his life. I was going to have to set up some kind of a truce for practical reasons. We were never going to be best friends but if we could just be civil to each other it would make the whole thing easier. It would also be better for Dad. The fact that his wife and his son didn't get on put Dad in a difficult situation and I am ashamed to say I believe that it ultimately had a detrimental effect on his health. If he knew we were talking that was one thing that he wouldn't have to worry about. Also I hate confrontation, we all do and I'm not a bully. Beverley is a small lady and with her history it would have been easy to take her apart. Not that she didn't deserve it, it's just that it wouldn't be an even fight. If I am honest I wish I wasn't the way that I am. I wish I was one of those heroic kinds of people that you see in the movies.

The real men who see the world in black and white, the 'never compromise, even in the face of Armageddon' types but I'm just not like that. Besides I have seen how that particular philosophy turns out. It tends to leave people who are self-righteous, lonely and though they may be cool in the movies in real life they are just sad. So I said "Hello Bev". She said "Hello Peter". and pulled up a chair on the other side of the bed.

What I didn't like about the new situation was how it became so normal so quickly. She was sitting on one side me on the other. At first she focused her attention on my Dad, she was concerned to see how he was and then she asked me how I was. It's not in my nature to be rude and so I told her and then asked her how she had been. Within five minutes it was as though nothing bad had ever gone on between us. Like the drunken phone calls and outbursts never happened. That made me slightly uncomfortable because they had and it begs the question how could she just sit there as if everything between us had always been hunky dory. I think that there are two reasons why. Firstly, I think that Beverley's problem was mainly with Lisa not me. She blames Lisa for the reason why we owed them so much money even though It wasn't Lisa it was me. I could say that she made me do it but she didn't and even if she had that would just be passing the buck and that is just weak. That's Uncle Billy.

My mother in law (Doreen) has a brother who is nine years younger than she is. Both of their parents died early and so Billy came to live with my wife and her family. He was sixteen at the time. Now this creates a very unusual dynamic for Dor. She is now both sister and mother. Billy had a string of girlfriends until eventually settling down with Sally. He might not have settled down with Sally but she got pregnant and that was simply what you did in those days. Over the coming years Sally has slowly but surely poisoned the waterhole to the stage that they no longer have any contact with each other. His kids barely talk to her and she doesn't see her nieces or any of their children. She cries every day. I know that people say that but she genuinely cries every day. If she comes round for dinner on a Sunday, we run a book on it. "Okay who had Dor crying at half past one?" The fact that she had open heart surgery three weeks before my wedding and has been on a pile of medication ever since may have contributed to waterfall of tears over the years but ultimately it is the fact that in one foul swoop she lost a brother and a son. Is Sally to blame for this? No, Billy is. Spineless git. Stand up to your wife. Tell her you're going to see your sister because that is the right thing to do. Sure you'll get a pile of grief when you get back but ultimately your wife may respect you more for it. Take responsibility for your actions and do the right thing.

The second reason is that I think that all the way through it Beverley was playing at it. She was never genuine; she doesn't know how to be. All of the crying and drinking and wailing was just seeking attention. She never actually felt it. I don't deny that she felt something. They were together for years but the way that she behaved was more for her benefit than his. She actually said to Dad once: "It's alright for you, you're the one with the cancer, you're going to die, I'm the one that's left behind". He told me that one morning as we travelled to the warehouse. Everyone I have told that just looks at me in utter disbelief. In truth, in that situation, there is a part of all of us that would feel this. But you don't say it. You don't wail and cry. You stay strong and you do your crying when they can't see you. That's love. Not the wailing banshee. That's just amateur dramatics.

Before I knew it the actress said let's go out for a coffee. I thought I'd rather not. Sorry. There I was standing outside the ward and she was telling me that she was frightened that he might not come out and I was thinking that if that was the case then all of this would be over. You think the unthinkable. You think that if my Dad dies at least I won't ever have to see this woman again. When I was sixteen I had a dream that I had a Ferrari and in the same dream both my parents had died. When I woke up my first thought that went through my mind was disappointment because the Ferrari had gone. I then laughed to myself at how ridiculous that thought was. Here I was thinking it for real. It doesn't make you feel good about yourself. We went back in and said goodbye to Dad and then I walked with Beverley out of the hospital. I suggested that we should visit at different times as this would make it better for Dad as he would have a family member around more of the time. We all know the real reason for this suggestion. As it was it was rather a moot point.

Ch. 12 The early morning phone call

It was quarter past five in the morning when the nurse called.
To most people this is like the middle of the night but I get up
at half five for work anyway and so I was awake. She said
"Your dad is very weak; I think you had better come in".
That's all they will tell you. You try to get more information
out of them but I guess they are trained that way. What they
should say is "You had better come in because your dad is
definitely going to die soon," but they can't because they don't
actually know that. Yes they do. I started to get ready.
Should I abandon work? I was heading into London anyway
so all I had to do was take the van to market where I could
leave it with earworm Nige and then I could take Nige's car to
Euston. What If I find out that he died in the extra time the
detour takes me and I could have seen him one last time if
only I had gone straight there? What if he goes on for days? I
have never been in this situation before, perhaps the nurse got
it wrong. I would go to work, pick up the car and head off to
the hospital, it's what he would want me to do. Then a bigger
thought hit me. What about Beverley?

          She lives five minutes round the corner from me and
she would have got the same phone call that I got. She would
currently be making plans to get to the hospital. That's if she
even got the phone call. She might be in bed comatose after a
heavy night's drinking. If that was the case then so be it, that
would be Karma but if she was sober she would be in a state.
She had just had the phone call to say that her husband is
dying, she would be fragile and confused. I didn't like the

woman but I was sympathetic to her plight. Certainly she would be in no fit state to drive or use the trains and the tubes. Or should I just go and make my own way. No one would blame me if I did, they knew the history between us and to be honest I was surprised that the thought had even crossed my mind but it had and now I had to work out what to do next. There is no choice. I would do the right thing. I called Beverley.

She answered and she was sober. She had also had the call from the nurse and she was getting ready and was going to drive to the station. I told her that I would pick her up and that I would take her with me. She was relieved and thankful and surprisingly I actually felt good about the fact that I had elected to take her. The thing is it is easy to help the nice people, it's helping the bastards that's the real challenge. You have to help the bastard's in the hope that it will rub off on them and that way bring about real change. In my experience this doesn't actually happen, they just stay bastards.

I travelled to Northall to pick up my passenger, then by van to Wilsden and then with the help of earworm Nige's mobile skip (honestly you have never seen a car like it) on to Euston. I parked by the British Library and me and Beverley did the short walk along the Euston Road to the hospital. Dad was there in the bed. His hair was flaccid and limbs were thin, in fact he resembled his mum just before she died.

My Dad once said that 'there is only one person in the world better than me and that's my mum'. He was joking, well partly but it is fair to say that my nan, Dorothy, was a

190

great woman. Her husband, my uncle Charlie, worked at Vauxhall. They lived in Luton, everyone worked at Vauxhall. He was an old fashioned hard working man who worked all of the holidays and overtime to pay for the house and provide security for his family and then soon after this was achieved, dropped down dead of a heart attack. This left my nan alone with the task of raising three children under the age of sixteen on her own. This she did with aplomb. She went on to live a long and happy life. Well the first bit was happy, she spent the last ten years in a home with severe Alzheimer's.

Cancer is a shit disease but there are shitter ones. At least with cancer you know what's going on. There is an argument that it is better not to know, ignorance is bliss but I don't go with that. Sure cancer is frightening but so is realising that you can no longer comprehend the world around you. It is also embarrassing and debilitating. You lose your independence as you can no longer be trusted in your own house and so for your own protection you are sent to a home which is effectively a prison that smells of piss and biscuits and there you are left to rot. No one comes to visit because when they do all you do is talk bollocks and they conclude what's the point of going as you are away with the fairies and that you probably don't even know who they are. My Nan's home was two streets away from my house and I never visited. I did at first but then when she got so bad I couldn't. To see her in that state broke my heart. I now know that I was wrong. I should have gone no matter how hard it was for me because what if on the inside my nan could understand me but just couldn't articulate it. My uncle Ian visited her every week. He lived twenty minutes' drive away and he wasn't even blood.

Now Dad looked the same way as my nan had done in the home. The appearance I could live with but what was more troubling was that he kept trying to get out of bed. He must have been on some strong pain killers because he was very disorientated yet he had one clear thought in his mind. He didn't want to be on the machines any more no matter what the consequences. He wanted to go home. I briefly entertained the notion but I knew in my heart of hearts that without the technology keeping him alive he would be lucky to make the lobby. We sat with him for about twenty minutes while we waited for the surgeon to arrive to tell us what the actual situation was. Eventually we were taken to a waiting room away from the main ward while we waited for the surgeon to arrive. I did a lot of displacement activity. There is only so much coffee you can drink so instead I spent my time looking in cupboards, sitting and then standing and then walking to the window and then sitting again. I also went to the toilet a lot but I think that this was partly to remove myself from Beverley. To be honest at this point I had put our differences over to one side. My Dad and her husband was dying and there are some things that are bigger than personal differences.

The surgeon came in with another consultant and a nurse. We sat down in a circle and the surgeon explained that there was nothing more they could do. What surprised me was how far they had gone before reaching this conclusion. They had considered doing both lung and brain operations but couldn't because his body was too weak and wouldn't survive. I've got to be honest at this point I thought 'really!' You don't need medical training to know when it's time to go. Sometimes I feel that the Hippocratic Oath is somewhat hypocritical. Perhaps my opinion was influenced by the fact that I knew that he didn't want to go on. The surgeon explained that he would never recover but the machine was keeping him alive. He stressed that it was the decision that they had made based on all the medical evidence and that we were not to feel guilty in any way. Still we had to decide when to turn the machine off. I looked at Beverley and she looked at me. Turns out after all it was my decision. I said "I know that you have done all you can and we are incredibly grateful, we'll turn the machine off today". Dad said to me once, as I'm sure many people say: "You won't let me end up like my mum, you will kill me won't you boy." We went back to the ward. We had one other person to wait for. My friend Ken was coming up to say goodbye for the last time. Dad had been a second father to Ken and it was only right that he should be there. He arrived after twenty minutes and said his bit. Then a strange kind of interval descends. How long is the appropriate time before you call the nurse and ask them to pull the plug? A decision had to be made and we were never good at long goodbyes. I said to my Dad "Okay dad I'm going to get you out of here, the only way I can". I called the nurse and said: "It's time". I promised my Dad that if it ever came down to it I would kill him. I never really thought that I would actually have to do it.

Ch.13 The machine stops

After they turn off the life support machine there is an indeterminate amount of time for how long the patient will last. I suppose it kind of depends on how strong they are and how much they want to go on. I hoped Dad would go quickly. Like I said we didn't do long goodbyes and you could genuinely refer to the time he had left as dead time. As a visitor you watch the life support machines like you are in a bookmakers watching a race. The heart monitor slows, then slows a bit more, then it goes up, then it slows again. Even at that point you still don't believe that it's real, that it is actually happening. You think that a miracle might happen. That he might start to rally and then whip his breathing mask off and say "let's get out of here." By next Monday we could both be in the warehouse drinking powdered cappuccino and playing pop master. Then the strangest thing happened. The only physical evidence I have to the existence of a transcendental soul.

Beverley and Ken were sitting on the left hand side of the bed, I was sitting on the right and I was looking at my Dad's head. That's when it happened. A wisp of smoke, similar to what you get when you blow out a candle, emanated from the top of my father's head. Genuinely happened. Now you think at that point the first thought that would go through your mind would be some kind of religious epiphany like 'his soul has gone' or 'he's off to a better place'. No, well not me anyway. I remember the exact thought that ran through my mind. I thought 'that's odd'. Now looking back on it I have questioned whether it actually happened or I imagined it. Perhaps I have created the memory to feel better about my father's death. I didn't. I definitely didn't create the memory and there is another reason that I am sure of this. I also remember the second thing that I thought and that again is not what you would expect. Seconds after I saw the wisp the nurse said: "He's gone" and I thought 'bloody hell those machines are good; they know the exact point that someone dies'. Now a puff of smoke doesn't prove anything. It doesn't mean that there is life after death. It doesn't mean that there is a heaven or that there is a god. I am not a religious person and I am not trying to convince anyone of anything. I'm just telling you what I saw and I really did see it. I know what I think. You make up your own mind. When someone you love finally goes, providing that they are not young and particularly if they are ill, it comes as a kind of a relief. It is as if their journey is finally over and now all is at rest. But of course it is not over yet. There is still paperwork to be sorted and death certificates to be obtained and of course, there's the funeral.

I helped Beverley with the funeral arrangements. I had kind of hoped that when Dad finally passed that I would only have to see her once more, at the funeral. The problem was he was my Dad and I wanted to make sure that it all went off okay so for that reason I had to be involved. I took her to the undertakers where we agreed what casket he should be cremated in and how many cars we would need. They asked what clothes they should dress the body in and Beverley decided to have him dressed in nothing but a red thong. She said that he would find that funny. It's not what I would have chosen but it was a closed casket so who cares. Besides she was probably right.

On the actual day of the funeral I went to Beverley's house on my own. It was decided that it was important that I should be in the funeral car and that Lisa, Molly and her family would meet me at the crematorium. I was nervous that morning. I was nervous as to whether anything would kick off. I didn't seriously believe that it would but you could never know for certain. The main reason that I was nervous was because I wasn't sure whether I would be able to hold it together as I had elected to speak. The reason I had chosen to speak is because I hate it when you are at a funeral and the priest gets up to talk about someone and it is clear that they have absolutely no idea who they are. I don't blame the priest. We complain about a lack of Christian values but none of us go to church. I know you don't have to go to church to be a Christian but the two sort of go hand in hand. Moreover, how is the priest supposed to give a heartfelt talk about someone who they have never met. They try their best but on more than one occasion I have been to funerals where they have got their facts wrong. I sit there as the priest does the eulogy thinking in my head 'he never worked there' or 'he did have a brother; his name was Steve'. For the service Beverley had decided not to go with a priest but instead to employ the services of a humanist speaker. This is a professional public speaker who will spend a good couple of hours talking to you about your loved one beforehand so they can compose an accurate account of the deceased. I am pleased to say on the day Sylvia did a fantastic job and got nothing wrong. She got nothing wrong because soon after she had spoken to Beverley she rung me with a view to correcting any potential mistakes, of which there were many. Sylvia was hard pushed to get any sense at all out of Beverley on account of her being smashed.

The funeral car left Beverley's house and proceeded on the half an hour journey that would take us to the crematorium. As we turned on to the main Dunstable Road we passed the warehouse and I thought of all of the Monday mornings we had spent up there lifting boxes and playing pop master. A warehouse full of boxes would seem very empty without him now. We arrived at the Crematorium and after greeting those who had come to pay their respects I went to join my family. I wouldn't be going into the crem with them as I was to be one of the pall bearers. I've never carried a coffin before. Coffins are heavy. Funny that a grown man in a six-foot-long solid wooden box. I don't know why but I expected it to be lighter, after all there are six people carrying it. The main man in the black suit sedately instructs you on how to handle and carry a coffin properly but you are still petrified that you're going to cause them to drop it. We took the coffin to the front and placed it upon the podium. When I turned around I saw that Lisa was leading the family towards one of the pews at the back of the crematorium. I went down to meet them and told them that they are my family and that they have as much right to be there as anyone else, in fact more so, and that I was standing at the front and that I wanted them to stand next to me. So there we were, spearheading the congregation. Beverley and her friends on one side and me and my family on the other. There were the usual openers and then my speech. it went like this:

197

"Thank you coming everyone. We are here to mourn the passing of my dad the market trader, and boy did he did love markets. I imagine that you've all seen the comedy series 'Only Fools and Horses', well my life was the live show. From an early age in our little flat in Marsh Farm in Luton I would get out of bed for school and make my way towards the bedroom door carefully avoiding the pile of kids Babygros that been carefully stacked along the opposite wall. I still find the smell of cardboard comforting; it reminds me of bedtime. From when I was old enough to work I would go with my dad. Every Saturday we went together to Newmarket and we would work happily all day and then on the way home listen to whatever album we both liked at the time. Kirsty MacCall, the Bangles, Queen and ELO featured heavily. On bank holidays we would work Fordom market together. It was in a farmer's field and when it wasn't a market the farmer used it to keep his cows in so we put a shovel on the back of the van for the obvious reason. Mum baked us fresh rolls and filled them with red salmon for our lunch and we always ate them before we had even got out of the van.

That was my dad he loved his work, he loved his holidays and he loved a party and he was good at it all. Although I have to say not every parcel he bought was a winner. I remember one particular line he brought. It was kid's world cup t shirts. They had a print of a football in the middle, across the top of the football were the words 'World Cup' and on the bottom of the football were all of the main teams of the time: Arsenal;

Manchester; Liverpool; Newcastle. It wasn't until I was unpacking them with Martyn the next day that Martyn said. "Pete, these teams don't play in the world cup". As it was they were one of our better sellers and we went back for a second batch. Another winner was the parcel of returns that we got from Bid Up TV. Eight pallets arrived of assorted sewing machines, mirrors, hoovers. What we couldn't work out was that if they were returns why they all looked so tidy and why they had individual stickers with people's names and addresses on. Well we put them out and they walked straight out of the door. I sold over thirty sewing machines in the first morning. It was a couple of days later when we got the call from Bid Up TV and the guy said to my dad:

"We need our stuff back".

"You can't have your stuff back" my dad replied. The other guy said, with a little more urgency,

"You don't understand; we need it back".

"No you don't understand, I've sold it".

Turns out the delivery driver had picked up the wrong eight pallets. The ones we got were not returns but fresh stock all waiting to go out to a multitude of customers".

It was at that point I paused

"I read this speech to Lisa and she said "that doesn't describe your dad to me at all". She said "Your dad was a kind and gentle man, he wasn't just about markets" and she's right he was. He listened to you when you were talking and was interested in what you had to say. He was always in control but he never dictated. He helped people and he never moaned about it. I remember one day at the warehouse when as usual he was trying to solve all of our problems for us I said "What about you dad? What do you want?' He replied "I just want everyone to be happy". Well it's a Monday morning,"

I turned to the coffin behind me and said

"and he's still got me lifting boxes. He was a kind and gentle selfless soul and I am going to miss him terribly."

I saw little of Beverley after that. I would have liked to have seen nothing at all but even when someone is dead and buried there are still practicalities. Paperwork that needs to change hands, there is the scattering of the ashes and so forth. The most annoying thing is that she is sober now. It was all just for attention. Once she realised that no one was looking, she stopped. Either that or she reformed herself after my Dad died. I can't help but think 'why could you not do it before? Everything would have been so much different'. Either way it's over now. As far as giving the speech goes I was nervous but nowhere near as nervous as I was the last time I had to do it. Oh yeah, I was talking about my Mum.

201

Part 3

Mum again

Ch. 1 Nigel

The second visit to Spain was nowhere near as scary as the first on account of the fact that it wasn't the first. I had already been over so I knew how the land lied and what to expect. This doesn't mean that it wasn't still scary and any possibility of moral support would be gratefully received. As usual the family volunteered their services but again I declined the offer. I didn't want to put them through any possible aggravation, molly had school and beside, we couldn't afford it. Fortunately for me I have very good friends, one in particular. My best friend Nigel.

Few people will be able to remember the first things they said to someone who later became a big part of their life but I know exactly what Nige said to me, it was: "Do you do magic?" Pretty cool introduction eh? Well not exactly. We were eleven years old and we were in the library of Challney High School for boys. It may have been a boy's school but it was still a state school, not a posh school and we had all just migrated from our junior schools with three hundred kids in them to one that held nearly two thousand. Understandably we were terrified. As first years we were convinced that it was just a matter of time before some of the fourth or fifth years descended upon us in the playground and kicked us to death. Half the pupil's in my class didn't turn up of the second day such was the fear. Nige was one of them. In truth the only reason I didn't feign illness on day two is that I was convinced that if I didn't go in on day two it would stand out like a sore thumb and I was sure to be killed on day three.

As it was on day three I found myself in the school library. We had an hour a week where we went to the library. The theory was that we could use this time to either do our homework or to sit quietly and read any of the library's many books. In truth we were all too lazy to do our homework and none of us were interested in the books so instead we spent most of our time screwing up bits of paper into small balls, chewing on them so that they became hard and then flicking them across the desks at each other with the help of a ruler. However, on the first lesson I actually thought that I may be able to use this time effectively so approached the librarian who stood by a door in the corner and hoping no one could hear me asked if she had any books on magic. At the tender age of eleven I was a keen conjurer. Now there were no cool magicians in my day. No David Blaines or Dynamo's. No, we had Paul Daniels. Say what you like about Paul (trust me in magic circles they used to say a lot more) but the man was a hell of a magician and I wanted to be able to do what he did. The librarian then replied, in a relatively loud voice "Magic books? Magic books? There might be some in the reference section". The whole of the library stared at me. That's it I thought, I'm dead. To my surprise nothing happened, at least not for a short time. Then when I suppose he felt an appropriate time had passed a small ginger haired lad approached me and said "Do you do magic?" We have been the best of friends ever since.

If you didn't know him better on the face of it, you might feel sorry for Nige. For a start he was adopted. Fortunately for him he was adopted by the best and most loving parents anyone could wish for. He was adopted as a baby and was told of the fact at an early age. This simple fact, a lack of belonging, can be enough to floor some people. Not my mate. He has taken the whole thing completely in his stride. Sure if you ask him would he ever consider contacting his real parents you can tell that there is an overhanging question that must plague all adoptee's. He would tell you that himself, but it doesn't define him and he certainly wouldn't ever seek to find out his real parentage while his mum is still alive, purely out of respect.

Nigel's mum is still alive. Unfortunately Gerald, Nigel's dad is not. When Nigel was sixteen his dad was diagnosed with Multiple Sclerosis. He was relatively fine for next five years or so and then he went downhill rapidly. Nigel lost his father when he was only twenty. Two weeks later Anne, his mother, told him that she had been diagnosed with the same disease. MS is not a contagious disease and the two cases are in no way related, it's just bad luck.

In some ways Anne had not been as lucky as Gerald. Her degeneration has been a long slow process. At first you become a bit unsteady on your pins, then you struggle to get upstairs so a stair lift is fitted, then you can't get up stairs at all. Nige organised having the garage converted into a downstairs toilet and bedroom. Later a hoist was added to help her into bed. Eventually she lost the use of her legs all together. The house was already converted but being in a wheelchair with Multiple Sclerosis makes it so much more difficult to get out. They bought her a special vehicle, affectionately referred to as the 'Pope Mobile' but even with that it's still not easy. Now her condition has worsened still.

205

She now only has the use of one arm and her posture has significantly weakened. This whole process has gone on for over twenty-five years and through all of this time Nigel has been a primary carer.

You remember that, like with Alzheimer's, I said there are worse things than cancer. MS is another. It slowly takes your life away while all the time you are completely conscious. It's kind of a negative image of Alzheimer's. If I had to choose one of the two I honestly don't know which one I'd pick. Lisa's nan also had Alzheimer's and her end was relatively pleasant, especially in comparison to my nans. Lisa's parents found her a home that smelled more of biscuits than piss and when we came to visit she would show us around and organise sandwiches for us. She thought that she owned the place.

I might not be able to choose between the two but I know which one Anne would choose. She would choose the one she's got. You see two years after Nigel was adopted Gerald and Anne had a baby of their own. Carol is Nigel's sister and from day one she has been one of the most important things in Nigel's life. Woe betide anyone who would dare to rubbish his sister. Thing is you would have no cause to, Carol's great and alongside Nigel they have taken great care of their mother, as a result she has been able to watch her family grow. Carol married Nathan and had a baby who they called Lucas, who is now seven. Anne never complains about her situation, although she sometimes finds the lack of movement frustrating. It is often things as simple as not being able to have a drink because one of the out of house carers have placed the cup just too far out of reach. She's a fantastic person struck by yet another shit disease, a position which is very much alleviated by having her family around her.

As an outsider it is all a big deal but Nigel has dealt with this stuff all of his life and to him it is nothing. He is clever and funny and when I was in shit financially he has always helped me and then when I couldn't pay him back when I said I would he would just say "Don't worry about it mate". Now I had to return to the dragons den and Nigel had volunteered to go with me. In truth I make the return trip to Spain all sound much worse than it was, let's face it, we were going on a jolly.

It wasn't the first time I had been on holiday with Nige. In fact, we had been on many school trips together. It was good that I was his best friend as we often ended up sharing a room and Nigel's snoring is second to none. Seriously, he's stayed overnight in sleep clinic to try to cure it. They even wrote an article about him in the Daily Mirror proclaiming that he had finally found a device that solved the problem. Had it fuck. I stayed over at his less than a week ago and he still shakes the house. Unlike most people it just doesn't bother me. If it wakes me up I just think 'What's that noise, oh its Nigel's snoring' and go back to sleep. As far as the device goes he had a vested interest in it. Every time someone followed a link to the manufacturers page, Google paid him ten pee.

He also came away with us several times on family holidays. Personally I love going on holiday just the three of us. It's the only time that you really get the chance to regroup as a family without any other external influences, like work or people, getting in the way. Thing is holidays can be an expensive business and when things started to go bad then I opened my mind to ways that we could reduce the cost. As it is Lisa's sister is single. She was married for several years to a very tall man who spent a lot of his time smoking dope and playing World of Warcraft on the PC so eventually it didn't work out and they divorced. Now she is in that strange land of the single holiday.

My mum told me once that one of the main reasons that you need a partner is that when you are a single woman the invitations stop. When you are in a couple you are not a threat because you have a husband but if you are a single woman on your own then you must be looking for a husband. Perhaps you are looking for 'my husband'. Therefore, you are now a threat and the invites stop. What can I say? Women hate women. The other problem of course is that people have families of their own who they also wish to go away with to get away from it all and so as a singleton the possibilities of holidays diminish. As a result, Jo was always up for a trip away. This is fine, I get on very well with my sister in law. She is very bright, great fun and has hollow legs which means that she can probably out drink me. The problem is that it does actually change the dynamic. Lisa acts differently when she is around her sister and I suppose so do I. Not in any extreme way, it's just kind of different. It's like if you ever go out for a drink with two good friends who come from completely different friendship circles. Everybody gets on fine but it all feels a little bit alien. If you want it honestly: I get jealous of the time that Lisa spends with her sister on holiday. I don't make a big deal out of it because I am not twelve but it is like Lisa has bought another one of her best friends along for the ride. Best way to square this circle is for me to bring one of my best friends too. Enter Nige.

Nige was single at the time and thus free to do what he wanted whenever he wanted. Actually although he is in a couple now he still pretty much does what he likes. Anyway the five of us worked really well on holiday. Like I said he's a funny guy. I remember one particular time that we were in Portugal and a group of German tourists asked me to take a photo of them. As they explained to me how the camera worked (it was one of those digital SLR jobs) I noticed Nige disappear off to the left at some pace. Then as I was framing the shot I noticed a movement in the top left corner of the frame. It was Nige. He had scaled the harbour wall and was slowly walking in to shot with big thumbs up in front of him and a massive grin on his face. I believe they call this photo bombing but I wasn't expecting it and all I could think of was that when the Germans got their camera back they would instantly look at the photo on the camera screen, see Nige and blame me and there was absolutely nothing that I could do about it. Fortunately, the Germans took it in good humour which was lucky really because by the time they realised I had started to laugh. I know this story doesn't really translate but I laughed until I cried for about ten minutes. I can honestly say that I have never laughed so much in my entire life. You had to be there. Now me and Nige were off to Spain. I was still nervous about returning but I was grateful to have him by my side.

Ch.2 Cudeca

The second visit to Spain also went smoothly. Mum had
always got on well with Nige (he literally is the kind of guy
that you could take home to meet your mum) and in many
ways the whole trip away mirrored the first. On the first day
we met for lunch and then Mum would go home and we went
back to the pension for siestas. We were tired from travel and
Mum was tired from cancer fighting and a multitude of drugs.
Then we met for dinner and afterwards Derick would take
Mum home because she was tired and me and Nige would
trawl the various bars of Fuengirola where I would drink San
Miguel and Nige would drink either Strongbow or Bulmers
which would make his conversation slur and increase his
chances of falling over, it's one of the cider fects.

On the second day when we met up Derick asked me
if I was free for the afternoon as there was somewhere he
wanted to take me. There is a place on the costa del sol, near
Tivoli World, called Cudeca. Certain things in this life are
wonderful and Cudeca is one of them. It's an organisation
completely funded by charity money where cancer patients
can go for respite care. Out patients go and meet other cancer
sufferers. Sound's joyous but who better to empathise with
you than your fellow sufferers. They have a wing where there
are nurses who take care of any wounds or sores that you
might have. They also have beauticians who will do your
nails and more importantly your hair and the most incredible

210

thing about this place is that fifty percent of the staff are English. The place treats Spanish and English alike but it was originally set up by an ex-pat who lost her husband to cancer and so created Cudeca so that no one would have to suffer the way he did again. There's a picture of the lady founder in reception. She is standing outside Buckingham Palace holding her OBE.

Me, Mum and Derick had an appointment with one of the doctors to discuss Mums condition. I left Nige back at the hotel and the three of us took the coastal road to Benamadena and to the hospice. The hospice was in a medium sized Spanish bungalow style building resting at the foot of the Sierra Blanca mountains. We parked in one of the few spaces outside and entered through the main doors, through reception and through another door at which point the building split into a kind of L shape. Ahead of me was the treatment room which comprised of a coffee room a beauty room and a rehabilitation room which was kind of a gym but not like any gym that you would imagine. Out to the left stretched a long corridor. To the left of the corridor lay a meeting room and doctors' offices and another reception for the in patients. To the right lay the rooms where the patients resided. Before all of this on the right hand side was a chapel. You were under no illusion why that was there. Derick spoke to the nurse on reception and we waited for the doctor to meet us. I'd like to say that it was peaceful but I fear it was just quiet.

The doctor met us and led us into his office where the three of us took seats in front of his desk. He explained what they did there and what would be available to Mum. Simple things like massages, hair styling and nails. The simple things that make us feel better, feel human. There was also the fact that while Mum was having her treatments she could be left there by herself. This would mean that Derick would have an hour or so to himself and for a full time carer this time is so important. I know that the situation between me and Derick was far from ideal but you also have to understand that the poor guy was doing all of this pretty much by himself. His family had all but left him to it and many of Mums golfing buddies were now noticeable by their absence. Serious ill health is like a magic spell; it makes people disappear. This is why hospices are so important. Not just for the patients but because they give the carers a break. Watching someone you love slowly die is a draining process. Add to that the fact that you have to organise all of the treatment and their need to constant care without respite, it would leave a young man exhausted, let alone one who was sixty plus with a heart condition.

Then the doctor went on to lay out what would happen at the very end, when Mum's condition degenerated to such a state she would no longer be in a fit state to remain at home. The doctor said when things got really bad they would bring her into Cudeca where she would get her own room and twenty-four-hour care. Then the doctor added "but that is a long way off yet". I was stunned. I thought 'what do you mean when she gets really bad, are you blind man, she's really bad now. Look at her she can barely walk, she can't wash herself, she can't even get in and out of bed'. What I should have realised at the time is that this man is an expert who has spent his life dealing with terminal cancer patients. She's really bad now, how little I knew.

In the evening the four of us went back for dinner to Mums favourite restaurant on fish alley. Aroma, owned by an Irish John Kelly. Still had the triangular plates. Mum did her best but the full on days were wearing her out. There is something really sad about watching someone in a diminished state of former glory. Mum would still make all the effort to get dressed up and put her make up on but due to her immobility and as a result the increase in her size she was looking less like my mother and more like a cartoon version of her. It wasn't like I could say that she still sounded like my Mum because the degeneration in her speech meant that her conversation was becoming increasingly more clipped leaving us to fill in the blanks. The meal was fine but we cut it short, it was obvious that Mum wanted to make the most of our time together but meals like this were becoming beyond her. We skipped pudding and said our goodbyes. I told Derick that I would visit again soon and that I would come by myself next time. It was fantastic to have support, what with all of the strangeness that was going on but there comes a time when you have to man up and get on with the situation as it actually is. It's not a string of weekend jolly's, it was Mum and her degenerating health. That was what this was really all about and she deserved my undivided attention so that was what she was going to get. With that in mind after saying our goodbyes me and Nige found a bar where we got befriended by the bar staff who shut the bar with us still in it and the five of us got absolutely smashed on a profusion of various shots until around four in the morning. I have been told that drinking is not big and it's not clever but I needed that drink. Besides I like a drink, I'm six foot one and I have a masters' degree in Philosophy, therefore drinking is big and it is clever.

I booked the next visit for about six weeks later. I used to talk to Mum, or Mum via Derick on the phone every Sunday morning and this time on going over I was going to stay with them. I wasn't sure how this would go down, particularly with the rest of Derick's family but I was assured that Jane would stay away and that Linda wasn't talking to him anyway. There were also certain advantages to staying with them. Firstly, I would only have to shell out for the flight which on EasyJet from Luton was cheaper than getting a day return to the seaside (how can that be that you can fly eighteen hundred miles for less than it costs to travel 60 miles on a train?) Secondly, I would get to see more of my Mum.

On one particular Sunday morning I was watching the news and an item came on that caught my eye. My Mum had friends in Spain called Phillip and Sheila and they had a special needs daughter called Sophie who my Mum was very close too. Philip was also my Mum's financial advisor and because of the particularly low interest rate at the time had advised that she invest her money in a medium risk investment off of the pacific rim. She lost the lot. Two hundred thousand pounds. It was her money and her choice although I still find it difficult to believe how my parents, who were very savvy with dough, managed to lose it all so easily but like I say, it was their money. Anyway I'm watching the news and there is a breaking story of a man in Spain who shot both his wife and his daughter before turning the gun on himself. The daughter had special needs and his wife suffered from serious depression. The whole thing was premeditated and he had written a suicide note before doing it. Then they showed a picture of Phillips house. You can google the story; it was in the Irish Mirror in June 2013. The only reason that I mention it is to try to get across how crazy things seemed at the time. I was in England receiving stories on national news of my mother's friend killing his family. It was like an unfunny version of the Truman Show. I spoke to Derick that morning before speaking to Mum and asked him if he knew what had happened. "Don't tell your mother". he replied.

I flew out to Spain a few weeks later. Mums house had changed dramatically from the house that it used to be. The downstairs toilet was now a shower/wet room and the living room was now also a bedroom on account of the fact that it now had a bed in it. All of this showed the significant change in Mum's mobility, stairs even with the lift were no longer an option. Mum and Derick had a general routine which I fell in with. We would watch the news in the morning, which due to the fact that they were using Jude's sky viewing card was from BBC Cornwall. I may have been in Spain but I knew what the weather was doing in Bude. Then we would go to the bar. Mum liked the bar because it got her out and there were often people who knew her or customers who had been coming to Spain for years that would wander in and say hello. Mum also liked the bar because it meant that she didn't have to walk anywhere. Like all of us Mum was proud and would only use sticks if she had to and the use of a wheelchair was as a last resort. I understand this. My friend Fred the Spread had an expression: 'Give a man a crutch and he will lean on it'. I never understood this expression at first but later I worked out that Fred was having a go at the doleites that you often see in inner city London. Young men who are perfectly capable of work but instead spend their time hanging around street corners perched on kids BMX's, smoking spliffs and drinking lager. Fred was old school, a true believer that you should do it all on your own and handouts don't actually help, benefits are actually detriments. Once you become dependent upon something you always need it and Mum was frightened that once she moved to the chair there would be no going back.

While I am with Fred and believe that you should do all that you can when you can, being adamant that you don't need help when you do creates a problem. We were sitting in the bar and I asked Mum if she fancied taking the short walk round the corner to the square for a coffee. Mum said no and that she was actually happy where she was. This wasn't true. What she actually meant was 'I would love to go and sit in the square but it's too much effort' so she would rather stay where she was. In a way the bar had become her crutch and I told her this. I said: "Okay look mum you've got two choices here. You can either sit in the bar every morning for the rest of your life, a prisoner to the same four walls or you can swallow your pride, get in the chair and I can take you out for the morning. We can go to the beach first, look at the shops and then maybe go to the square for a glass of wine. End of the day I am here to visit you and I will do whatever you want. If you want to stay in the bar all morning that's fine, I'll go round to the shops and get a pack of cards and we can spend the morning playing rummy, it's up to you". I went round the corner and brought a pack of cards. When I got back to the bar Mum was sitting there, in her wheelchair.

From that point Mum used the chair and it enabled her to get out a lot more. If she had waited until she had to use it as her only way of getting about it would have just meant that she would have done a lot less. It wasn't that she didn't try to regain her ability to walk again but let's face it, with a lump like that growing in the middle of your cerebral cortex it was never going to happen. It's like I always say: 'If at first you don't succeed try, try, try again, then give up. There's no point being a bloody fool about it'. Ironically I had to have the same conversation with Fred. He got lung cancer and could no longer walk any distance at all but he was too proud to do anything that made him look like an invalid. I told him to get himself a mobility scooter, it was either that or spend the rest of his life looking at the inside of his flat. Two weeks later he came zooming down East Street market on a brand new scooter with an oxygen cylinder on his back. Alas it got little use as he died soon after. On the flip side if you know anyone who needs a nearly new mobility scooter? Never mind.

The fact that Mum's life had become more sedentary and the fact that her eating habits remained the same meant that she was now becoming rather heavy. I don't blame her for this. Eating is fun and due to her illness there was not a lot left in my Mum's life that was fun. On the first night of my stay the three of us went out for a curry and I had to get Mum in the chair up a narrow steep concrete ramp. It took me all of my might to do it. Mum in the wheelchair was the weight of a pallet of coke and the damn thing steered like a cow.

More to the point the only reason that I had the luxury of moving Mum in the chair was because of Derick. He had been the one to get the chair, albeit with Mum's money, but he was also the one who got Mum to the car and then packed up the chair, then got her into the bar and then did it all again in reverse. He was the one who washed Mum every day in the wet room. He was the one who took her to the toilet. He did all of this, day in day out every day without break and with very little respite. He did things for my mother that I never did. I offered but she said that she never wanted me to. I have a child of my own and so I understand, It's a matter of dignity. There are some things that you do for your children that you never want them to have to do for you.

On the evening of the second day Derick was going to work in the bar. This would at least give him a break from the routine of caring. It's a bizarre situation when you find yourself going to work for a rest. Mums friend Lucy had come round and the three of us were going to watch a film together. I have met Lucy many times and consider her a friend but that afternoon there was a strange atmosphere in the house. It's hard to explain. It's like when twilight comes on and there is a colour shift. Things that are red suddenly appear blue. Everything is the same but also in some way different. It felt like that. About ten minutes before leaving Derick suddenly felt bad about leaving us and said that he could get someone else in to cover the pub but Mum was absolutely adamant that she would be fine and that he should go. You know when you know someone so well that they are up to something but you also know that it is wise not to say anything? Mum was up to something. Soon after Derick left for the bar Mum's next door neighbour Julie appeared. Of course she did, you need two independent witnesses if you are going to make a will.

It turned out that Mum had also been concerned about what was happening with her finances. She may have been undergoing the effects of a horrific disease but one of the side effects of cancer is not stupidity. Although she was no longer able to log into online banking on her laptop, when you can barely string a full sentence together you've got absolutely no chance of remembering a ten-digit alpha numeric code, she still knew what was going on. Derick didn't exactly mask it. He would say things like "I've moved this money from your mums account into mine because if I need to get her anything it makes it easier" or "I have transferred the log book of your mum's car into my name". He didn't even give a reason for that one. It wasn't that I didn't care about what he was doing, but he was looking after my Mum and it wasn't like I really had a lot of choice in the matter. Still as I have already said the whole thing did leave a rather unpleasant taste in my mouth. Seems it felt the same way for my Mum too. I have also learned that when people are dying there are practicalities that must still be attended to. For their own peace of mind people want to tie up loose ends. Maybe not everyone. I'm sure many people die and leave their affairs in an absolute mess, which is a bit of a 'well I'm dead so it's your problem' kind of attitude. As far as my clan were concerned they were very much in the 'I will sleep a lot easier when I know that everything is in place' camp. So a last will and testament document was produced, the blank kind in the plastic sleeve that you get from the local post office. Ironically enough it was an English one which means that Mum must have gone to the trouble of asking one of her friends to bring it back from the UK. Alongside all of Mum's Spanish assets she also had a flat in England, the one she bought as somewhere to stay when she came home as staying with me would mean a civil war. As time passed Mum came to the conclusion that for the amount of time she came home it would be better to rent the flat and stay in Bellows Mill when she came back. The other reason that she bought the flat was as an investment/pension for her old age. Now a bit of a moot point.

So I came to find myself in Mum's front room with two of her best friends and a sheet of A4 paper from the post office. I asked Mum what it was all about and she told me in broken sentences that she was concerned about the way that her money was disappearing. Mum and Derick had discussed the matter and it had been decided that the flat in England should be left to me. Still she had her fears that after she died Derick may forget this fact and she wanted to make sure that he couldn't have the flat in England too. What she actually said was "He's had enough". And so me, Mum and her friend Julie proceeded to fill in a last will and testament document on my mother's behalf. Just for the record if you do ever have to make a will, get a professional in. You wouldn't rewire your own house so what makes you think that you can do what solicitors do. The post office one will do the trick but you will make school boy errors and at the end of the day a proper will, will speed things up and makes things so much easier. I guess here I should put the number of a firm that I recommend, I might get some kickbacks.

We navigated the questions as best we could and when it was completed we all agreed not to mention it to Derick. It was merely an insurance policy. If everything went according to plan, then he need never know. If however, when all was said and done he decided to pull a stroke I would be in a position to stop him. As we were discussing Mum's assets I asked her "What about the house in Spain mum?" She simply looked at me and said "That's Derick's". There you have it. Clarity. Everything is what it was and we all knew where we stood. There is a relief that comes with clarity. Even if you are hoping for one thing and it turns out completely different, once you know where you stand you can move on. Wipe your mouth and walk away. I am going to stop talking about money now. As I have said it is a dirty subject and after all this story is not about dough, it is about my parents and their partners and what happened to them. What happened next was that Julie left and me Mum and Lucy sat down to watch Chocolat on DVD. I thought that she would really like it but when it was over she said that she thought that it was boring. Then she said that she had difficulty following what was going on. Things weren't getting any better.

Ch.4 Reunited

Things had settled down between me and Derick and yet it still came as some surprise that at the end of one of my usual Sunday morning phone calls Derick asked "Peter, do you think that Lisa and Molly would consider coming with you on the next flight out, I know that your Mother would love to see them". I said that I was sure that they would be more than happy to come which was a lie because I wasn't but I figured that if they weren't up for it then I could just make some Mickey mouse excuse which we would all know wasn't true but would just whitewash over it and then things could carry on just the same. Fortunately, they were both more than up for it. The flights were booked, Mum had offered to pay and this time rather than stay at the house, Mum didn't want Molly to see the way she now had to live her life, we stayed at one of Derick's two flats. Yes, despite constantly pleading poverty in addition to owning the lease on a bar Derick also owned outright two flats but I said that I wasn't going to talk about money anymore.

Looking back, it is easy to tell that our minds weren't right. On the morning of the flight we got to the airport in plenty of time. We sat and had a nice bit of breakfast and then I went to the chemists while Lisa and Molly disappeared off to Smiths to get some magazines for the journey. After all we had nearly half an hour before the plane was due to take off. It was only when they came out of Smiths that me and Lisa looked at each other horrified as we realised that you are supposed to be on the plane an hour before take-off. We were running towards the departure gate when our names were called over the tannoy as the gate was now closing. We made it just in time. They laid on a whole transport bus for the three of us just to get us to the plane and we did the walk of shame down the aeroplane aisle to our seats knowing that we may have just caused the entire plane to be delayed because I was in boots looking for toothpaste.

Fortunately, the plane took off on time and we got to Malaga when we were supposed to. I usually got the train from the airport but because there were three of us we got a taxi to the bar. It was too early for Mum and Derick to come and meet us, her daily washing, toilet and dressing routine had become rather a long one. We got to the bar about twenty minutes before them. We went in and got drinks and I thought how strange it was. We were doing what we always did before Mum's diagnosis and at that moment it felt the same. You have a feeling that she would turn up just the way she always had and the whole thing would be just a bad dream, albeit a very long one. This was not the case. We were sitting on one of the small white plastic garden tables when Mums Renault pulled into its usual parking space just across from the bar. Derick retrieved the wheelchair from the boot and I rushed across to help. Derick had to collect a few other things from the car so I left Mum and Derick there and started decanting some of Mum's usual paraphernalia back to the bar. When I got back to the table both Lisa and Molly were crying. Mums degeneration had been gradual and I had been there to witness it but they had not seen her for the best part of a year and for them the shock was just too much. Nevertheless this was not the time for this. I looked at the two of them and said "No. Not now. You know the rules, you pull yourself together, for her sake." And they did.

Funny thing is as human beings we are very capable of adapting to new situations really quickly and within a matter of minutes we were all inside the bar talking like old times. For Mum you could say they were very old times as her one word sentences made her sound somewhat Neanderthal but nevertheless we were chatting. We stayed in the bar for a bit and then they took us to Derick's second flat. Previously we had always stayed in the first flat. It wasn't as nice as the second but was right in the heart of things, directly above the bar and across the road from the sea. I love the sea. I love the noise that it makes and the way that it stretches out for what seems an eternity. Back in the days when I was taking money I was lucky enough to go on a cruise. We had a cabin with a balcony I remember sitting on a chair with a beer in my hand and my feet up on the railings watching as the boat ploughed through the infinite blue towards our next destination. The only sounds I could hear were the waves and the sound of my wife and daughter in the cabin behind me getting ready for the evening meal. It is the happiest memory I have.

The second flat was bigger and in a better decorative order than the first and we had the use of a large communal pool, not that we would use it. We were here for reasons other than swimming. It also didn't have the aura of death about it, a certain portentousness that had come to inhabit my mother's house. This evoked mixed emotion within me. Staying in a place away from the mechanical armchair and the

225

commode, the constant reminders was definitely less of a strain but this also served as a constant reminder that my Mum was down the road coping with this while I was a few miles away doing nothing. This time I was there just for the company and bearing in mind the company was her grandchild I think that that was enough.

In the afternoon we all had a siesta. We were tired from the travelling and Mum was just tired, pretty much all of the time. I don't know if it was the cancer or the drugs that they gave her to keep it at bay but in truth it matters not, the end result was the same. In the evening we got ready and took the short walk down to the main square where we stopped for a coffee and a brandy. There is an old fashioned place just off the main square that looks like something from a French Noir movie and specialises in coffee, brandy and churros. Churros is basically a straight plain dough that is full of calories and tastes of nothing. It is effectively a carrier. You dunk it in your coffee or your hot chocolate whilst drinking brandy and smoking throat wrenching Spanish fags. It's a very Spanish thing to do. They do it all of the time, particularly around eight in the morning where for many it is a staple breakfast before the working day. I recommend it. Unless you are going on to drive or operate heavy machinery. That night we were going to meet Mum and Derick and we had elected to eat in the bar which was unusual as it was something that we never did. The bar was a simple affair, in no way fancy. Outside was a Taldo, a gazebo like affair that had to be constructed every morning before the bar was opened and taken down again at the end of the day. Once up there was just enough room for four, four seated square white garden tables beautifully decorated with chequered plastic table cloths. As you entered the bar, past the gas bottles, to the left was a bench seat with three small round wooden tables and to the right the actual bar stretched the whole length of the room. It couldn't have been longer than fifteen foot. The whole thing was a modest affair that at full capacity held less than thirty people. Yet it had three tellies, for the football. I hate tellies in pubs. No matter what is on you find yourself drawn to them. I have gone out with friends in the past and caught myself watching Gloria Hunniford chastising builders. Pubs should be sociable places you go to catch up with those dear to you. Not somewhere you go to watch MTV with the sound down.

That night we sat in the bar. It was reassuring for Mum to be somewhere where she knew, and where she could get to toilet facilities that they were not far away. Mum now got very little warning when she needed to go and had had to start wearing nappies as a result. Just another way in which the indignity of cancer helps to destroy your life. Still the evening was lovely. We ate burgers and fish and chips respectively. Molly played at being a barmaid for the evening and it absolutely smashed it down with rain. Entrenched in our little bar, we were cosy.

We met up again for lunch the next day. They wanted to take us to a little beach resort near Benamadena. On the beach was the old town hall, a relatively small building that had the appearance of a life boat station. It had been converted into a restaurant but most importantly it was very wheelchair friendly. There was a wooden pathway that led from the outside terrace, straight across the sand and into the sea. They even had special wheelchairs that were designed to submerge. We asked Mum if she wanted to go in but she declined. I have a theory on this. If you are born with a disability or you acquire one relatively early on in life you are more likely to accept it. You learn how to cope with it and how best to overcome it. Our Paralympian's are a testament to that. When you get a disability in a situation like my Mum's you think of it as one step closer to dying, another door that has been shut on the person who you once were. Either that or she thought that the water would be cold. Instead we sat in the sunshine outside the small town hall and enjoyed seafood and sangria on what turned into a very pleasant afternoon.

That evening we were set to go out. Mum rarely did this now but we were going home the next day and she wanted to make a night of it. On the Fuengirola front, opposite the statue of the Lady of the Sea was a proper old family run Italian restaurant. It had been there since Derick had taken over the bar more than twenty years previously and with a name like Pirozzoli as I'm sure you could imagine he was a big fan. Unfortunately, it would not be open for much longer. Unable to cope with the rising rents it was about to fall victim to the souvenir shops and English breakfast bars that litter the fronts of many Spanish resorts. We were going there. On the whole eating your own traditional food whilst away on holiday is not something that I understand. You go on holiday to Greece and then go out for a curry. You're in Greece, eat tzatiki. You're only there for two weeks you can have a curry when you get home. Of course it was different for Mum and Derick, they lived there and it was where they wanted to go and so we were more than happy to oblige. I have a photo of that night. You know in the film the untouchables where our four heroes are enjoying shorts and cigars and a reporter comes in and takes a box flash photo of them around the table, it is like that. Although not quite like that, one of us was certainly not untouchable. I still look on it fondly never the less.

It was a short walk/wheelchair ride back to the bar. Up a side street and then left on to fish alley, the bar was at the end. As we meandered up the restaurant covered street Derick said to Molly "Molly why don't you push your grandma?" Molly took the chair and then a couple of seconds later Moll said "Come on grandma". and started to sprint, chair in hand, off towards the bar. Derick was shouting " be care full Molly". and Mum was screaming. She wasn't frightened, she was happy. When we got to the bar and said our goodbyes. We were on the morning flight and much as she would have liked to Mum would never be ready to see us off. We helped get her into the Renault, collapsed the chair and put it with the commode in the boot. As I stood waving watching the car turn right onto he costal road I wondered if my Mum would ever see her Granddaughter again.

Ch.5 Barret Homes

I went in a helicopter once. I know I keep talking about planes but once I also went in a helicopter. It was much earlier in my life when me and Mum were living together in the flat in Marsh Farm. They were building a new Barret housing estate up the road and as a publicity stunt they brought in the Barret helicopter, the one that they had on the adverts at the time. I saw it come in to land as I was riding around the estate on my Grifter. I rode to the top of the estate and approached a well-dressed man in a grey suit and tie to ask him what was going on. He told me that they were giving free ten minute rides to the first few people who arrived. "Great" I thought. But you had to be accompanied by an adult. Well that was that one out. I knew what Mum would say, she would say what she always said, no. Still there was this great big whirling thing next to me and they were giving rides for free. I had to go for it. I pedalled back to the flat as fast as I could, dumped my bike on the pavement stones outside, opened the door with the key on a piece of string around my neck and ran into the kitchen.

"Mum, mum, there's these guys up the road and they're giving rides in their helicopter for free but you have to be accompanied by an adult. Can we go mum? Please. Please".

"Alright". She said. I nearly fell over.

"I'll just put some make up on".

I waited eagerly in the kitchen. There would only be so many slots and if we waited too long we would miss our chance. I contemplated riding up on my bike to hold a place in the queue but I knew that this would be pointless, it was only a place if my Mum was with me. Mum emerged from the bedroom ready to go and I lead her by the hand like a dog desperate for a walk towards the waiting helicopter. The walk to the top of the estate seemed to take an eternity. When we got there, to my amazement, we were the first in the queue. It turned out that adults are not too fussed about riding in a helicopter and all of the other children were having the problem that I thought that I would have.

The smartly dressed man opened the back doors and we got in and buckled up. The pilot took off straight upward and I looked out of the window as the world became small. He then took us on a loop over the estate. Over the flat where I lived with my Mum, over my school and the park with a helicopter of its own, albeit one made out of colourful metal bars, over the Purley Centre shops where Mum used to send me for bread and back towards the new estate. Before landing the pilot took the helicopter high into the sky and then put it into a steep exhilarating nose dive, only pulling up at the last minute bringing it safely to rest where it had started. I got out that helicopter and I was as happy as I was the time I walked out of the cinema after just watching Star Wars.

Good old Mum, she didn't always say no.

Ch.6 Day time telly

On my next visit over Mum had become bed bound.
Something was wrong with her which meant that movement
was now painful. Even getting out of bed to get into the chair
in front of the telly had become too much of an effort. By this
stage Derick had secured the services of two, part time carers.
A combination of Mums fading mobility and her increase in
size meant that Derick was no longer capable of giving Mum
a shower on his own. Now on alternate days either an Irish
lady, who was nice, or a thin teacher type who was also nice
but also a bit nutty would come in and give Derick a hand
washing and dressing Mum. They would also stay with Mum
so that Derick could go out for an hour or so to give him a
break. He would usually pop down to his youngest daughter
Jane who also had a bar on the front. Jane had come back into
the fold and would now come over to the house to help out.
Mum liked Jane, she made her laugh.

For the meantime the carers had been put on hold.
There was nothing they could do while Mum was bed bound
but this also meant that Derick was getting no respite
whatsoever. His whole life had been consumed with looking
after my mother. It was time for me to take over and give him
a break for a while. Derick left for the day and Mum lay in
bed in the front room, dozing in and out of consciousness.
Sitting on the sofa and without a book on the go I had little
else to do than immerse myself into the world of day time
telly and although Mum was half asleep I elected to stick to
her viewing schedule as at least the sound of familiar

programmes might be comforting. Oh my god. My viewing schedule went something like this. BBC news. From Cornwall. Then Angela Rippon in some programme about workmen who rip you off. Homes Under the Hammer. At that point Mum had properly fallen asleep and I really couldn't take it any longer and started binge watching Breaking Bad on my kindle with one headphone out so I could hear Mum if she needed anything. Then on her resurfacing we watched the end of a programme where a familiar looking orange coloured man looked at antiques, Loose Women, more binge watching Breaking Bad while Mum drifted off again and then Tipping Point. This is a real highlight. For those of you that have never seen it they have actually managed to make a game show that is based upon those penny machines that you used to get in arcades when I was a kid. If you look up the definition of banal in the dictionary all it says is 'Tipping Point.' And to the best of my knowledge it's still running. Then it's The Chase. I Don't mind that, I like Bradley.

That night I told Derick that I would sleep downstairs with Mum. Derick did this every night. They had a house full of bedrooms and Mum slept on a bed in the lounge while he slept on the sofa. As he explained to me he could never get a proper night's sleep because he would always have one ear open in case Mum needed him. Soon after going to bed Mum started groaning saying that she was in pain and that she wanted to be turned over. The correct way to do this is to get what they call a slip-sheet under her and then the pulling of the sheet would turn Mum over. Problem was I couldn't get the sheet under Mum without causing her pain so I elected in my infinite wisdom to just grab her and turn her quickly as one sharp pain would be better than lots of little ones. I was wrong. She screamed in agony and Derick came bounding down the stairs in his Y fronts to find out what was wrong. I told him what had happened and he just said "never mind son, best I take it from here". He never did get his unbroken night's sleep. I slept upstairs and Derick was where he was every night by Mum's side. There are many things that weren't right about the situation but there is one thing that cannot be denied and that is the fact that Mum could not have had better care than the care that that man gave her.

It was clear that Mum's health was deteriorating rapidly and as a result I made an effort to get out to Spain more frequently, both to spend more time with Mum and to give Derick more support. On my next trip I felt like I was getting flying off to a fine art. I was only ever out for three days at a time and I had my drag along case so I didn't have to queue up to check in my bag. It also meant that I didn't have to wait at the carousel at the other end all in all saving me about an hour which was more time that I could spend with Mum. In addition to this as you reach the top of the stairs at Luton airport, before you start the twenty-minute queue for the x-ray machines, to your left is a gate that says priority lane. Not many people realise that it is there and most of those that do don't know how it works. It was Nige who clued me up on this. Basically opposite the priority lane gate is a row of machines into which you either put your bank card or four pound coins, the machine spits out a receipt, you take the receipt to the gate and you go through to a separate x-ray machine with a very small queue. I'm not the richest man in the world but I am willing to invest four pounds if it means that I don't I have to spend the next half an hour in a queue kicking a case along the floor.

The other thing about Luton Airport is that as you enter the foyer there's a guy standing there with a bucket. Not just any bucket but a bucket that says Brain Cancer charity on the side. What are the odds? Well there's no way that I can walk past that. I would always throw any spare pound coin's in that I had. A guy once said to me that I gave him more money than he had received all morning. I just smiled and thought if you knew the reason I was travelling you wouldn't be quite so surprised. This particular morning had not gone smoothly. The taxi had turned up late and I was kind of up against it time wise. I threw all my cash at the brain cancer people and reached the top of the stairs to find that all of the card machines for the priority lane were out of order. I approached the lady at the start of the normal queue and asked

"What's happening with the priority machines?"

She replied "The card ones are all offline, the only ones that work are the ones that take coins".

Coins, something that I no longer had. I said "Great, I had coins but I just chucked them all at the brain cancer people downstairs, never mind I'll just join the queue, I still have time".

"Oh bless you". she said and then I felt bad because it was as if I had said it to elicit a response. As I walked past I thought what I always thought, 'you've no idea but that's okay, it's not your problem'.

Two minutes into the queue a young guy from customs came and tapped me on the shoulder. I thought 'this is not my morning; I've been flagged up for something. He's going to take me off to a room somewhere and shove a rubber glove up my bum and of all the times that I had taken this trip this was the one when I most needed to be on time'. But he didn't escort me off to a room. Instead he took my left arm and led me to the blue rope that separated the normal from the priority-lane. He lifted the rope and let me through. The lady that I had spoken to must have told him what I did and she had got him to let me bypass the queue. The guy must have thought that I was mental because I started welling up. I can handle all of the grief and the misery but the kindness of strangers is too much to bear.

Ch. 7 Chemo comes to an end

The reason that I needed to be there on time was because
Derick had phoned me and told me that I needed to come over
because Mum had an appointment at the hospital. She had
decided to stop the chemo. Unlike Dad, who had had the
chemo stopped on him because it simply wasn't working
anymore, Mum had decided to stop because she just didn't
want to go on any longer. It was clear that she was never
going to get better and all the treatment was doing was
prolonging what was becoming a very undignified life. In
short she had had enough. I flew into Malaga airport and
instead of taking the train to Fuengirola I jumped in a taxi to
Malaga general hospital where I met Mum Derick and Lucy in
the canteen. Lucy was not just there for moral support, she
was there because she spoke Spanish like a Spaniard and on
this visit to the doctor there could be no mistakes.

We moved from the canteen down to a basement part
of the hospital where we were ushered into a small waiting
room full of mainly Spanish patients. Normally in Spain if
you are walking down the Fuengirola seafront or in one of the
Cabapino supermarkets you don't feel out of place. There are
English people everywhere. Hell when you walk down the
seafront most of the signs are written in English trying to sell
you egg and chips. Here we were definitely out of place but
we weren't made to feel uncomfortable. You could see it in
people's eyes, they didn't say 'what are you doing here?' They
said 'I know why you're here'. We all had one thing in
common. There is a kind of bond between people who are

that sick no matter what the nationality. A certain empathy that is felt among fellow sufferers and those who look after them. Doesn't matter where you come from, we all go through the same thing. Eventually we were called in to see the consultant who spoke little English, which strangely I found reassuring. I thought rather than focusing on learning a foreign language he has concentrated on medicine so he must really know what he is doing. His English wasn't great but enough to explain to Mum that there were other courses that they could try and that they hadn't given up hope that Mum could still make some form of a recovery. Mum listened to every word the man said but only had one word to say in return. She simply said "no".

There are many things that life teaches us and at this point, being a student of the great philosophers I turn to a higher order mind: Bob Hoskins. After he died Bob Hoskins daughter made a list of the things that he had tried to teach her:

1) Laugh. There is humour to be found everywhere, even on your darkest days there is something to joke about.

2) Be yourself. If someone doesn't like you they are either stupid, blind or have bad taste. Accept who you are, you've got no one else to be.

3) Be Flamboyant. It's who you are and always have been. Be eccentric and unique. Don't try to adapt yourself to someone else's view of normal.

4) Don't worry about other people's opinions. Everyone's a critic, but ultimately what they say only matters if you let it.

5) Get angry. it's okay to lose your temper now and then. If anger stays in, it turns to poison and makes you bitter and sad. Get angry, say your piece, then let it go.

6) Whatever you do, always give it a good go. Don't be afraid of failure and disappointment.

7) Be generous and kind because you can't take it with you. When you've got something to give, give it without hesitation.

8) Appreciate beauty. Take pictures and make memories. Capture it, you never know when it will be gone.

9) Don't take yourself too seriously. People who take themselves too seriously are boring.

10) Never ever, ever, ever give up. Keep on punching no matter what you are up against.

11) Love with all of your heart. In the end, love is the only thing that matters.

Wise man Bob but he got one wrong. Number ten. Yes, keep punching but also know when it's time to throw the towel in. Mum knew It was time to go. The fat lady had sung or at least she would of if she could remember any of the words to the songs anymore. That was mean but when you are sitting at a word processor recalling what your mother went through, doing your best not to just break down in tears, humour sometimes helps. Like Bob says even in your darkest days there's always something to joke about.

On the way back from the hospital we were due to stop at a tapas bar that Mum loved, she could still enjoy food and although it didn't help her on her pins, or with her bladder, she did still enjoy the occasional glass of wine. In the car on the way to the bar Mum desperately tried to get out a sentence. It took her several attempts but she was determined and she managed it eventually. The sentence was "I just want to die". What do you say to something like that? What I said was "I think that we are all well aware of that mum but it doesn't actually work that way. Besides you can't die yet, we're going for tapas".

After lunch when we finally got back to the house. Me and Derick got Mum out of the car and walked her, each of us holding an arm, to the front door. I was supporting her as Derick found the key. It was then that she fell. She just went and once it started there was no way to stop it. Problem was once she had fallen we couldn't lift her. It was like trying to lift a motorbike. Mum was on the floor groaning not through pain but through indignity while me and Derick heaved to no avail. It would have been funny if it was funny. There we were in the middle of the day and there were no neighbours there to help. Other than next door, they weren't that close to any of their neighbours anyway. At one stage Derick contemplated calling the paramedics to come out to help us lift her. The thought of Mum stuck on the stone floor for an hour waiting for the paramedics was enough for me to find the extra strength inside myself and I pulled her to her feet. We got her inside the house and settled her in the armchair. The relief on us all was tangible. Derick stopped pushing her to go out after that. He had always encouraged her to get out, to keep her active to stop her just atrophying in front of day time TV and he did this tirelessly everyday with very little help from anyone else. He did this for his own sake as much as hers. He did not want to lose the woman that he loved.

Turned out that Mum would get to see her granddaughter again. I got the phone call from Derick to tell me that Mum had become very ill. She had been taken into Cudeca and now had very little time left. Derick asked whether Molly would come over with me on the next visit as Mum would like to see her Granddaughter one last time. We didn't stay in the flat this time. I wanted to be as close to Mum as possible. I didn't want to have to rely on anyone else for transport and I wanted to be able to spend as much time there as I could. Lisa found a small hotel that was about a ten-minute taxi ride away from Cudeca. We got to the hotel around ten, checked in and then got straight in a taxi to the hospice. Up until now I had only really been in the wing of Cudeca that dealt with day patients. Only once had I been through the doors where the beds were. I told the receptionist that we were there to see Vicky Coath and after finally working out who I was talking about (it's rather an unusual surname) she directed me through to room six. We went through the double doors, past the small chapel on the right, past the nurse's station on the left and through to Mum's room on the right. The room was very spacious with minimal decoration. There were two beds in the room and I can only assume that it was geared for dual occupancy. At the moment it was just Mum in the room and I hoped that would be the way that it stayed. Cudeca is a wonderful organisation, it gives its services for free, run purely on donations and I was grateful for its existence but it was going to be the last room my mother ever saw and from a purely selfish point of view it would be nice if she didn't have to share it.

Sitting at a small table opposite Mum's bed was Derick and the Irish carer lady and we met with normal friendly greetings. To be honest Mum didn't look that much different from the last time I had seen her but for Moll and Lisa the change was more dramatic. Not that this made any difference as the family rose to the occasion with the usual cries of "Hello Vic" and "How are you doing grandma?" Mum was clearly pleased to see the family but by now she was in the last throws of her grade four terminal brain tumour and her conversation was all but gone. Derick confessed that the reason that he brought the carer with him to the hospice was because otherwise you just end up sitting there on your own in silence. He said that at least if there is someone with you, you can have a discussion with them and you can still involve Mum in the conversation by occasionally saying "isn't that right Vic?" There was plenty of other entertainment for Mum but she had gone past all of that. Mum had her stereo radio but she didn't want it on. There was also a large modern flat screen telly on the wall opposite the bed but apparently now the noise of the TV irritated her. No more Tipping Point for me then.

Derick and the carer left about fifteen minutes after our arrival and about half an hour after that I said to Lisa and Molly that they may as well make a move too. Mum had seen them and they had seen her. As far as I was concerned I just wanted Mum to know that they were there for her and for them it was a chance to say goodbye but there was no need to

243

labour the point. Also for most of us we don't know how much time we have left with the ones we love but I knew exactly how much time I had left. Two and a half days. That was it. You know when you are a kid and you get the six weeks' summer holiday. At first it's great, then in the middle you get a bit bored and you kind of wish that you were back at school, then when you get to the last few days they are the most precious days in the world. I had jumped straight into the last few days and so I wanted my Mum all to myself. Besides I had a plan.

I knew from previous experience that Mum was going to find the conversation difficult but I didn't want to just sit there in silence. I wanted Mum to know that I was there and I wanted her to hear my voice so I borrowed an idea from Dudley Moore's character in Arthur. I was going to read to her. When his butler Hobson got sick and went into hospital, to keep him amused Arthur read him Hamlet. I wasn't going to read Shakespeare, that really wasn't Mums cup of tea. Instead I picked a book that Mum used to love as a young woman: 'All Creatures Great and Small'. The plan worked. I sat on a chair by the side of the bed, in shade away from the hot Spanish sun and read chapter after chapter about the adventures of the ill-fated vet. At the end of each chapter I asked "Shall I go on, mum?" And that was how we spent our day together, me reading and her listening and occasionally mustering up the odd word or two, although by now this was a near on impossible task for her. We stayed like that until at the end of chapter nine when I said: "Shall I go on, mum? " and Mum said "no". She was tired. I said I'll let you sleep now mum and I'll be back with the family tomorrow". and kissed her good night.

The next morning we got to the hospice early, which as it turned out was a bit of an error as Mum now spent a lot of her time sleeping. As she was still asleep we waited in the chapel. It was then that Derick walked in accompanied by Jane. This lead to a rather tense situation. Bearing in mind that the last words I had said to Jane were: "I'll pass you over to your dad because I don't want to fucking talk to you". this could be tricky. There was an eerie pause while the girls eyed each other up and then there was a second or two of silence as my wife and Jane measured each other up, as if trying to work out how this was going to go but then both said "Hello" and "How are you" and within ten minutes they were talking about Jane's kids. It was a relief; this was not the time for war. The rest of the morning went very much like the previous day. Derick and Jane stayed for half an hour or so and then when they left we said polite goodbyes. I hugged Jane and thanked her for all of the time and effort that she had put in with my Mum. At the back of my mind I thought that it would be good to have another ally on this side of the channel, especially with what was inevitably going to come.

Lisa and Molly hung around for a while talking to Mum and then they all left the two of us alone for the rest of the afternoon. Once they had left and me and Mum had a quick chat. I had talked at her for a bit while she listened then I decided to carry on with the story. I don't know if you are familiar with 'All Creatures Great and Small' but it is a bittersweet affair. Most of the stories are quite up-beat and

245

amusing but not all of them. Long and the short of it is, if you are reading Herriot to a cancer patient for fucks sake don't read chapter eleven.

It starts with James entering the house of a small white haired gentleman who had recently lost his wife and all he had left in the whole world is his dog. You can see it coming already can't you. The guy has called James in because his dog has become sick. The old man tells James what a wonderful dog he has and how he is normally so full of life but recently he has been off his food and is a shadow of his former self. He says to the good natured vet 'I hope you make him better soon'. James, who let's face it, has some experience in the matter is clearly intrepid as to what he is about to find. He turns the dog over to find that its stomach is distended and on feeling the dogs' tummy identifies a growth. He turns to the old man and gently breaks it to him that his dog has cancer and the kindest thing would be to put him out of his misery. The old mans' lip trembles as he says 'He's going to die."

His lips trembled! I was in absolute tatters. Believe me that small exert does not even begin to illustrate the full emotional impact of the whole chapter. I'm reading to my dying mother knowing that our time together would soon be over and I'm reading about some bloke who's only companion in the whole wide world is about to be put to sleep. I managed to finish the chapter, choking back the tears and doing my best to hide my upset from my mother. When I got to the end I said to Mum "Should I go on mum?" and she said "No." I went "No! I'm not leaving it there. Surely the next chapter can't be about a cow with a brain tumour." It wasn't. It was about the vets overbilling some farmers. I finished the chapter and kissed Mum goodnight.

That night I decided to read ahead. I knew that I had very little time in the morning because we were on a relatively early flight but I wanted to see Mum one last time. Fortunately for me it was about Mrs Pumphrey and a fat dog called Tricky Woo. She was always a favourite on the television series of the book and the whole thing was all very light hearted. The next morning I got to the hospice early and Mum was still sleeping. I didn't know what to do. We had very little time left together but I didn't want to wake her. So I just sat there. It was a very strange feeling. The most precious moments that we had left and I was powerless, sitting still as time poured like sand through my fingers. I stared out of the window at the beautiful gardens and fish pond and wondered if she would wake at all. She did. We spoke for a while and then I carried on reading. I only had enough time to read the one chapter and this made the whole thing so much harder. I knew how long it was because I had already read it the night before and so with every passing paragraph I drew closer to the moment when I would see my mother alive for the last time. I had to keep fighting back the tears as I didn't want my Mum's last memories of her only child to be that of a gibbering wreck. I finished the chapter and I have to confess that I think that she wanted me to read on, but I was becoming such a mess by then and I had to meet up with the family and catch an aeroplane. I still beat myself up about that. Every time I think of our last moments together I think that I could have done one more chapter, I could have

247

pushed for just a little more time but I didn't. We never did do long goodbyes. I kissed her on the forehead and told her that I loved her and then I left. On the way out I sat in the chapel and cried like a small boy.

We returned home and a couple of weeks went by and nothing had happened. I even started to think that there was a possibility that I could get out one last time. I could carry on with the book. Hey if I went out for enough time I could even have a go at finishing it. That was until a summer Tuesday morning when at about half past five in the morning the phone rang. It was Derick. Mum was dead.

It was over and all that was left now was to lay Mums body to rest. This was going to be interesting. I was going to fly to a foreign county to go to the funeral of my mother and stand beside a family of which at least one of whom actually hated me. And I was going on my own. The family had offered to go with me but I had already decided that it was better that they fly out to Spain to see Mum while she was still alive rather than go out to look at her in a wooden box, what would be the point of that? Of course they could have done both but money was still tight and to be honest I didn't want to put them through any more grief. I would do this on my own. I would be staying with Derick for the whole time of what would be my shortest trip of all. He had offered to put me up and to be totally honest I actually thought that this was rather a nice gesture. Mum was dead and he no longer had any real reason to keep up appearances. He loved my mother very much and this would be a very difficult time for him, a time when I thought perhaps he would want to be surrounded by his family. Obviously if this was the case then I couldn't be there, that would be an impossible situation. I had prepared myself for what I had expected to be a very lonely affair. Me on my own in a small hotel room in Fuengirola staring at the wall but that was not to be the case. Better the devil you know. I had never spent any time with Derick on my own before. I would fly out the day before the funeral and fly back on the earliest possible flight the day after. I didn't want to be out there any longer than I had to, after all, my reason for going was gone.

Derick picked me up from the airport and took me to their home. It was just the same as it had been. The bed was still there in the corner, the electric armchair was still facing the telly, even the commode on wheels was still behind the sofa. There was only one thing missing, the most important part of all. We didn't stay around the house for long. Both of us found that we didn't really want to be there, not in that situation, not without Mum. Instead we went to the bar just to make sure that everything was alright, we went to the golf course where the reception would be held to check that everything was in place for the following day. Then we headed off to Jane's bar where we were due to discuss the arrangements, music and flowers and so forth. I must confess to some degree of trepidation about this as we had only seen each other once since the fateful night when she had called my house and I had told her to fuck off. I need not have worried, Jane was perfectly lovely. I had never been to her bar before and it was much bigger and more impressive than Derick's which was not so much a bar, more a reasonable sized room with a tent attached. I think it helped that Jane had had a lot of contact with Mum before she died and that Mum and Jane got on. The three of us sat on one of the round chrome tables while outside the sun shone and the Mediterranean Sea lapped upon the yellow sandy beach. Jane told me how the service would go. They had arranged flowers on my behalf, white lilies, just like the ones I bought her that day in the square. They had sourced the songs that Mum had wanted, 'Hold On' by Wilson Phillips (she always sang that at karaoke) and 'Crockets Theme' by Jan Hammer. There were hymns as well, I requested 'All Things Bright and Beautiful' on her behalf. I thought it would be fitting: 'All Creatures Great and Small'. Lastly we discussed the order of service, during which of course I was going to speak.

Now this one was the big one. For a start pretty much no one there had ever met me before and most of them had only known Mum for the latter part of her life. Also I had never spoken at a funeral before and I was going to start with my Mum's. In at the deep end. When we got back to the house I started composing my speech. I had been thinking about it since I had heard the news and the strange thing is that when you try to come up with individual moments that help you define your relationship with a person it's actually very hard. Most of the times we spend with the ones we love are very esoteric, or just don't translate. Or you simply just forget. Try it now. Think of someone who you are really close to and try to think of some of the best moments that you spent together, ones that would translate to others in the form of a story. It's actually harder than you think. Nevertheless the moments came. The speech slowly came together and I walked circles around the shared swimming pool in their communal garden reciting it over and over again. This was a piece of advice that I had got from my mate Darren. He kind of inspired me to speak at the funeral as I had already seen him speak at his fathers and I thought it was so much better than having some stranger do it. I asked him how he got through it without breaking down and he told me that he had rehearsed it so many times that he had become desensitised to it. Now this was going to be a tricky balance. Too little rehearsal and I would fall to pieces, too many and I would sound like a robot. As with all things in life a solution presented itself. What you have to do is keep reading the speech out over and over again until you can read it through to the end without crying.

The morning of the funeral was a beautiful blue day. Of course it was, its Spain, they are pretty much all beautiful blue days. I took to walking around the pool once again, piece of paper in hand talking to myself to make sure that I would get it right. At the request of the minister I had typed the whole thing out properly in case when the time came to it I fell apart and was unable to do it but the hard copy was somewhat inadequate. I didn't make the effort that I should have done because I already knew that I was going to do this. As late as possible I got ready. I had the only proper shave that I have had in the last five years and then kind of wished that I hadn't because without any facial hair whatsoever you can clearly see that weak Coath chin. Then it was time to put on the suit. It may be hot out there but it's a funeral and you wear a suit. Black suit, white shirt, black tie, shoes polished. Weddings, funerals, christenings all the same, always dress with respect, don't turn up like a gypo.

Me and Derick would drive to the funeral together, just the two of us. At first I thought that I might be expected to be in a car with Derick and his family, including Linda. That was never going to happen. As it was they do it differently in Spain. The coffin is already there when you get to the chapel and so there is no procession. I asked Derick if he was okay with it just being me and him on the way to the chapel and he said of course. All the way there he told me stories about the things that he and Mum did together, the holidays that they had taken. We passed the Miraflores golf club of which my Mum had been lady captain and didn't we know about it. She never stopped talking about it. She was like the woman in Little Britain who claimed to be Molly Sugdens bridesmaid. And golf people are strange. They don't use letters to communicate they talk in numbers? "I was on the seventh and I was going to use a three but instead I used a five. What does that actually mean? We also passed the hole on the golf course where Mum had got a hole in one three times so there was a prime opportunity for him to tell that story again. I didn't mind. Derick told stories while wiping away his tears, he was clearly going to miss her terribly.

The chapel was a modern building on the outskirts of Fuengirola. This kind of surprised me as given Derick's catholic background I expected an old, austere cathedral with a pious priest. Instead it was a simple square affair with large glass windows, pale walls and stone. Best of all due to the large overhanging concrete veranda it was cool. A smart suit is all well and good but the look is somewhat compromised if you look like you've just walked through a car wash. We milled around under the veranda for a while. Mum's friends from the golf club approached me and told me that they were sorry for my loss, Jane's family talked to me, Linda's pretended that I was not there. Even my mother didn't like Linda. I asked her once on one of my visits over when she was not too far gone. I said:

"You don't like Linda do you mum?"

"No". came her usual garrulous answer.

"Why?"

"She's too black and white". she replied.

Eventually we filed into the chapel and me and the Pirozzolis stood in the front row, me on one side of the pew, Linda on the other. The music played. Not all of my Mum's taste in music was that bad, at a different time it would have been early Motown or Kate Bush instead of the incidental music from 'Miami Vice' but that was what she wanted, what can you do. Then the time came for me to speak, the minister beckoned to me and I stood up and took the podium, it went like this:

"Good morning everyone, thank you all for coming. It's difficult to know what to say at a time like this but I thought that I would tell you a couple of stories that best described my mum. Many of you know mum from the Miraflores golf course where she had served as lady captain and where on the fifteenth hole she got a hole in one three times. Suffice to say that she was not always that proficient. I remember one time when I had just got back to the house and I heard a cry from the garden, "Peter, can you come here a minute".

I walked round into the back garden and found my mother in the middle of the lawn, practising her swing. I stood beside her and uttered words of encouragement like "very good mum".

"Watch this" she said. She drew back her club, swung through and belted me right round the head with it. Neither of us had worked out that if you stand in front of a golfer taking a shot one of the consequences would be a golf club round your ear. I saw stars and staggered back somewhat disorientated.

"Are you alright?" She said. And then laughed. It was a nervous laugh as she was frightened that she might have hurt me. As it was I was fine and I learned to be far more careful around people armed with clubs.

Another time that springs to mind was when my parents took me to Disneyland on holiday. If anyone ever tells you that it never rains in Southern California they are lying. We were there in February and it hammered down. As a result the queues for the rides, even the big ones were relatively short. I wanted to go on Space Mountain but I was scared to go on my own. Neither of my parents wanted to go on. My Dad was useless at theme parks because he was afraid of heights and mum was little better. Mum being her usual supportive self said "If you want to do it you can do it on your own because I'm not going with you". All through the twenty-minute queue to the top I wondered whether I would go through with it or chicken out at the gate. The moment came and mum asked.

"Are you going on or what?"

"Yes" I said "I'm going on".

"Okay" she said "I'll come on with you".

Relief washed through my body, I would not have to go it alone. We got into the cars, the protection bar came down and then we shot off like a rocket into the dark. I was screaming with joy and as the car dipped and swerved. Then I noticed that mum wasn't not so much shrieking, more whimpering and muttering under her breath "ohh, I don't like it" and "make it stop". I was having a wonderful time but my mum was terrified. I spent the rest of the ride consoling her and telling her that it would be over soon".

Then I paused. It was my about Schmidt moment. The moment in my speech where I could put everybody straight on what had really gone on, how Derick had systematically robbed my mother, a woman who he wouldn't marry when it was thought that he would go first but who when he realised it would be her, acquired her bank accounts, house, car, and anything else of value. Do think I did it. Did I hell.

I continued.

"I would like to thank all of you who visited my mum and took her out. Ill health is not easy. Movement is difficult and conversation requires patience and often guesswork but I know that the times that she spent with her friends at the golf club or at the seafront made her final days brighter.

I would also like to thank mum's carers and the people from Cudeca. I say people but I should say angels. We would roll her in and her face would light up met by phrases like "hair and nails today?" "a bit of reiki?" and "yes we will remember to do your moustache". To you I am forever thankful.

And I ask you all to spare a thought for Derick. In my many visits to Spain I have witnessed the love and devotion that he showed my mother. Something that I should add she never failed to point out. She often told me how good he was, normally after she had the hump with him about something or had made him run up three flights of stairs to see if the towels were dry yet. No one should have to care for the one they love in such a fashion and he handled the whole thing with kindness and an unwavering conviction of which he should be proud. You see it's alright for me. Tomorrow morning I get on an aeroplane and fly home to the woman I love. He will never see his again. I ask you to support him in his time of need, just like he supported my mother.

Finally, I ask you to remember my mum during the good times. Remember her lemon meringue pie or her sticky toffee pudding. Remember her smile in the bar or on the golf course. Remember her direct and often cutting wit. Or just remember her as a kind woman who was your friend, which is the way that I think of her".

Epilogue

So it ended. I got on an aeroplane and flew home to my family. The whole thing was finally over. There was of course the matter of Mum's estate to work out. Basically Derick got practically everything. The house in Spain, the car, the contents of her bank accounts. I got the flat in England. I did have to use the will that we created on that fateful night but I never mentioned it to Derick because at the end of the day what's the point. Carrying anger and bitterness will just leave you angry and bitter. You are permitted, in time of great danger, to walk with the devil until you have crossed the bridge. Did I walk with the devil? I doubt it. I have come to realise that we all think that we are right and a lot of the time it is all just a matter of perspective. Not always, somethings are certainties but there are times when sound arguments can be made for both sides. Ultimately the final word lies with Wilko Johnson, guitarist from Dr Feelgood. At the same time as my parents were dying from terminal cancer so was he. He spoke passionately in an interview and said: "When I look back on my life I realise that I spent so much time worrying about things that really didn't matter". and this is the crux of it all. You can spend your life getting hung up on the detail or you can focus on the things that really count and it's really not that hard to work out what they are. My Dad said that his only regret is that we never properly played together. This was partly my fault because like I said I am not that good a musician but now I realise that that's not important, it was the doing it together that was important. The best things in life are the ones that you can't buy.

Don't spend your life in regret. I spent too much time thinking that I am not doing enough or that I could have gone out of my way more. I have questioned whether the friction between my family and both of their partners added to the stress to their lives and ultimately may have made their time of suffering harder, even hastened their demise. Both of my parents told me that they loved me and that they were proud of me and these are the things to hold on to. After the event it is easy to lose focus of the way things actually panned out, how strange they were and the unbelievable things that happened. Ultimately all you can really do is the best that you can with the information that you have at the time. What's done is done and the past is where it belongs, move on. After all, as my mate Nige says: "You only get one ticket to the gun show". The whole thing was like living in a part of the twilight zone and looking back on it is like looking back on a period of my life when I was on a massive amount of mind altering drugs. I can't even begin to estimate what effect it has had on us as a family but at the end of the day we did the right thing. I made sure that despite a large amount of crazy my parents knew that I loved them and that I was there for them no matter what.

I sold the flat, paid off my debts and did some long overdue jobs in the house. The money that was left meant that we were fairly comfortable for a year or so. We had a couple of family holidays and did our best to lick our wounds and regroup. It was fun while it lasted but the money has all gone now. I may be poor again but I saw it all through to the end and now that it is all finished my soul remains intact. Besides I have the solution to my poverty. I'm going to write a book.

The End

'- DAD. I may or may not have been tooooo intrigued and had to start reading. I got absolutely captivated and read the whole thing...then became massively disappointed when it ended and there was nothing left to read. Keep going your writing is exceptional and I will be the 1st to read your book before you become a published writer .xxx'

There you go Moll, I hope you liked it.

19342494R00151

Printed in Great Britain
by Amazon